"Don't look at me like I'm crazy!"

Sam exclaimed. "I just meant it's not like you'd have to stay married to Ray. You'd just have to marry him for a while."

But I have a boyfriend. I have a life! *Carrie thought.* "That's nuts!" she cried.

"I don't know," Sam said with a shrug. "If I needed to do something really, really big to save your life, or Emma's life, I'd do it. That's all I'm saying."

Carrie and Emma looked at Sam in astonishment. Sam, the one who doesn't care about politics, is actually in favor of me doing this? Carrie wondered.

"Sorry," Carrie finally said. "I love Ray, and I'll help him any other way I can, but I can't marry him. That's final."

"Not as final as it will be if he gets sent back to Matalan," Sam said softly.

Sunset Deceptions

CHERIE BENNETT

Sunset™ Island

SPLASH™

A BERKLEY / SPLASH BOOK

SUNSET DECEPTIONS is an original publication of The Berkley Publishing Corporation. This work has never appeared before in book form.

SUNSET DECEPTIONS

A Berkley Book / published by arrangement with General Licensing Company, Inc.

PRINTING HISTORY
Berkley edition / June 1993

A GLC BOOK

Splash is a trademark belonging to General Licensing Company, Inc.

Sunset Island is a trademark belonging to General Licensing Company, Inc.

ISBN: 0-425-13905-0

A BERKLEY BOOK ® TM 757,375
Berkley Books are published by The Berkley Publishing Group, 200 Madison Avenue, New York, New York 10016.
The name "BERKLEY" and the "B" logo are trademarks belonging to Berkley Publishing Corporation.

PRINTED IN THE UNITED STATES OF AMERICA

10 9 8 7 6 5 4 3 2 1

—a mon mari Jeff, qui j'adore—

Sunset Deceptions

ONE

"Sam, help me!!!" Carrie mock-screamed into the telephone, as she surveyed the scene in the Templeton's kitchen. From behind her came the voices of four-year-old Chloe and thirteen-year-old Ian, mid-fight.

"Down girl, down!" Samantha Bridges's voice came through loud and clear. "Calm yourself, girlfriend."

"You stink!" Chloe yelled at her big brother, who in response opened his mouth to show her some half-eaten corn flakes.

Carrie turned away and looked at the wall clock. *Nine in the morning. How can it only be nine in the morning?* she thought. *It feels like I've been awake for hours.*

"Sam, remember what I said about how I

1

loved children, and how I hope to have four or five of my own if I get married?" Carrie asked plaintively, ignoring the ruckus at the table behind her. "I take it all back."

"I knew you'd wise up eventually," Sam said with a laugh. "To what do we owe this revelation, you nineteen-year-old child-hater?"

"Give me back my troll doll!" Chloe was screaming. Ian was holding Chloe's troll by its green hair and swinging it above her head.

"Just that—hold on a sec," Carrie said. She turned her attention to the breakfast table. "Ian, give Chloe her troll!" she chided Ian Templeton, keeping an eye on him for safety's sake. "Sam? You still there?"

"Would I desert you in your hour of need?" Sam joked.

"Yuck," Carrie said. "Ian just dumped something yellow into Chloe's milk—I don't even want to know what it is."

"So, be careful when you do the dishes," Sam snorted. "Isn't being an au pair great?"

"Right now I'd rather be sweeping up behind the horses in the Thanksgiving Day parade," Carrie replied ruefully. "Look, just wanted to remind you that Graham's on Phil Donahue's show this morning. You want to come over and watch with us?"

"Sure thing," Sam replied. "The monsters have a tennis lesson this morning, so I'm free until noon." Sam was referring to the fourteen-year-old Jacobs twins, Allie and Becky, whom she called the monsters because of their often atrocious behavior.

"Great," Carrie said. "Don't bother knocking. You'll find us in the family room."

"Where you'll have both the kids bound and gagged in the middle of the floor?" Sam joked.

Carrie laughed. "I wish," she said. "So, I'll see you later." She hung up and went back to the kitchen table.

"I'm not drinking my milk," Chloe said, as Carrie sat down with them. "There's yellow stuff in it." She pointed at her glass with one grubby finger.

"Fine," Carrie said. "Just eat your eggs."

"Okay," Chloe said gratefully. "Is my daddy really going to be on television this morning?"

Ian spoke up. "Yup," he said, "on *Donahue*.

3

It should be really good. Maybe Dad'll mention my band."

Fat chance, Carrie thought to herself. *Phil Donahue is interviewing your father because he's Graham Perry, world-famous rock star, not because he's Graham Perry, father of Ian Templeton, lead singer of the pre-pubescent industrial-rock group Lord Whitehead and the Zit People, whose music sounds like a chain saw trying to cut through the Empire State Building!*

"I wish Mommy and Daddy would come home," Chloe said wistfully. "They come back tonight, right Carrie?"

"You got it," Carrie said. *And not a moment too soon,* she added to herself. Graham and his wife Claudia had been in New York for the last three days on music industry business—something about Graham having to meet with some executives from his record label—and Carrie had been in charge of the two Templeton kids from morning until bedtime. *The kids were pretty well-behaved the first day or so, but it's been downhill ever since,* she assessed. *I guess that's why they*

4

call it a summer job instead of a summer vacation.

"Well, it doesn't matter," Ian said.

"What doesn't matter?" Carrie asked him.

"Matter if Dad mentions the Zit People on *Donahue*, of course," Ian said brightly. "The way my band is going we're gonna get a ton of publicity on our own. Probably even have a label deal in a year or so."

Carrie laughed. "It's good to be optimistic, Ian," she said. "Now finish your cereal." She pointed at the nearly-full bowl in front of him. Miraculously, Ian actually picked up his spoon and started eating. Carrie looked at the clock. Nine-fifteen.

Graham and Claudia get back at nine tonight, she thought to herself. *Then, I'm going to sleep for two days straight, and then spend two days in Billy's arms. On second thought, maybe I'll switch the order of those activities.*

Because all of her time had been taken up with Ian and Chloe, Carrie hadn't had a free moment to see her boyfriend, Billy Sampson, leader of the popular local rock group Flirting With Danger. *I really miss him. Really.*

5

"Is Daddy on TV yet?" Chloe asked. "Because I'm ready to watch. Look Carrie, I finished everything."

Carrie pulled herself out of her reverie about Billy and looked at Chloe's plate. It was clean.

"Good for you, Chloe!" Carrie said, reaching for her dish. "Why don't you go watch some TV, and then Ian and I will come in to watch your dad with you?"

"Okay," Chloe said. "But first I'm going to put on my special hat."

Special hat? What special hat? Carrie thought. *I don't even want to think what that's all about.*

"You do that," Carrie said. "We'll meet you in the family room." She looked at the clock again. Nine twenty-five. *This day is never going to end. Never!*

"Ladies and gentlemen, welcome to the show," said Phil Donahue, as the camera came right in on his face.

Carrie, Sam, Ian, and Chloe—wearing an Easter bonnet she had evidently found in one of her mother's closets—were sprawled out on the floor of the Templeton's family room, watching the big-screen television set.

"Where's Daddy?" Chloe said, a concerned look on her face.

"Ssssh!" Ian said. "He'll be on in a minute."

Carrie watched as Donahue made some short opening comments about how rock and roll had changed the entire world. "And now," he said, "I want to introduce the man whose music has changed the face of rock and roll forever. Ladies and gentlemen, please welcome a living rock legend, Mr. Graham Perry!"

The crowd on TV went berserk with cheers and applause as Graham walked onto the set. He was dressed in his concert clothes. Instead of the torn jeans and T-shirts sported by most rock stars, Graham had chosen a different style—he wore an exquisitely-tailored Italian black tuxedo, a French silk white tuxedo shirt, and red Italian patent leather shoes. With his long, wavy brown hair and chiseled features, Graham looked fabulous.

"Nice uni," Sam said approvingly, shaking

her head up and down so that her long red hair moved sexily, "I wouldn't kick him out of my—"

"Sam!" Carrie hissed, indicating the Templeton kids with her eyes. "Just watch the show, okay?"

"Sure," Sam said, in mock-chagrin. "You got it."

"It's Daddy!" Chloe yelled happily. "Hi, Daddy, I see you!" They all cracked up.

The kids sat in rapt attention as Donahue interviewed Graham, tracing the course of his career from the early days singing in bars at the New Jersey shore for tips, all the way to his most recent concert—a benefit show in California where Billy Joel was Graham's opening act. The interview was highlighted with film clips, Graham's own reminiscences, and Donahue's often probing questions.

"To what do you attribute your longevity in the business?" Donahue asked Graham toward the end of the show. "I mean, rock acts come and rock acts go—"

"I've been very lucky, haven't I?" Graham said.

"So, you think it's just good luck, Mr. Modesty?" the host teased.

"Partly," Graham replied easily. "And maybe that I'm always willing to try new things," he added.

Phil nodded. "And how does all this success affect your family?" he asked. "There's . . ." he looked down at his note cards.

"My wife, Claudia, and my two kids, Ian and Chloe," Graham said. "I'd say they help keep me going when the going gets tough."

Ian and Chloe screamed together in joy. "That's us!" Ian said proudly. "We're on *Donahue*—"

"Sssssh!" Sam said. "He's still talking about you."

"—is four, and Ian's thirteen," Graham said.

Donahue stood up, wandered into the audience as was his custom.

"This is when the audience gets to ask questions," Sam explained, shifting to get more comfortable on the pillow she was leaning on. "I used to watch this show all the time

9

when I worked at Disneyworld. Breakfast with Phil," she joked.

Donahue walked up to an overweight matronly woman with ten tons of makeup on her face, dangling day-glow earrings on her ears, and a too-tight floral print polyester pantsuit on her bod, and he thrust the mike in her face.

Sam made loud siren noises when she saw the woman on the TV screen. "Emergency, emergency!" she shouted. "Call out the fashion police. Give her a life sentence!"

"Sssssh!" Carrie said. "I want to hear what she asks."

The overweight woman took the mike and stood up. "Graham," she said breathily, her pointy earrings dancing dangerously, "you're my favorite musician in the entire world. Can I give you a kiss?"

The camera swung to Graham. "Uh, sure," he said diplomatically. Like a shot the woman was out of her seat and waddling down the aisle, her arms open as if she were about to take a flying leap at the stage. Graham stood up and offered her his cheek.

The camera came in close on the woman, who, instead of kissing Graham's cheek, actually grabbed him, hugged him tightly to her massive bosom, and even tried to thrust her tongue into his astonished mouth before he could pull away.

"*Eeeee-yew!*" Sam yelled.

"Gross! Gross! Gross!" Ian cried out. "Totally diz-gusting!"

"I can't even look," Carrie said, hiding her eyes.

"Where's the barf bag!?" Sam said loudly, looking around the room in mock-desperation.

"Why is that woman kissing Daddy like that?" Chloe asked. "Mommy won't like it!"

"No kidding," Sam laughed. "And your daddy won't like it either. I don't think there's a man alive who would like it!"

"No more kisses!" Donahue announced, as the woman ran triumphantly back to her seat. The whole audience exploded in laughter. Then he ran up to the top tier of the audience where a a very thin woman, dressed entirely in black, was waiting to ask Graham a question. Donahue handed her the mike.

"Graham," she asked, her voice marked by a thick Texas accent, "when I saw you on TV a few weeks ago, you looked to be about ten, maybe fifteen pounds overweight. Now that I can see you live, you're even fatter than that! How do you account for it?" The woman waited expectantly for her reply.

In the Templeton's family room, Sam dug Carrie in the ribs and giggled. "Let's see how he answers this one!" she said.

Graham laughed ruefully. "No wonder my wife's been trying to put me on a diet!"

"These people, have they no shame?" Carrie asked rhetorically. "Anyway, he's got a great body."

"Hey, when you're famous, you're fair game," Sam said matter-of-factly, "that's just the way it is."

"Time for one more question," Donahue said on the screen. "Okay, over on the side, yes, you there!" He dashed to the far side of the studio and handed the mike to a young woman about Sam and Carrie's age who was dressed in a very hip-looking red leather jacket and a short black miniskirt.

"Two points on the outfit! I want it." Sam said.

The woman took the mike from Donahue.

"Graham," she started, "there are a lot of kids my age using cocaine. Everyone knows you've been in and out of rehab at least twice. What advice can you give us, and why can't you seem to quit?"

The studio audience went deadly silent. At the Templetons', Carrie looked over to Chloe, to see if she was paying attention. Her eyes were glued to the screen, just like Ian's and Sam's.

Finally, Graham answered. "My advice?" he asked the woman. "I'm qualified to give advice? I'm a musician, not a social worker or a psychologist."

"Yes, but you can speak about your own experience," the young woman pressed.

"Okay," Graham finally said. "Here's my advice. Don't start. Because I started once, and now I wish I never had. I'm clean now, but it's a struggle—every single day of my life." The audience exploded again into applause.

13

Credits started to roll over the screen. The show was over.

"Wow, big points for honesty," Sam said, looking over at Carrie.

"Major," Carrie agreed. "I'm proud of him."

"Me too," Ian said.

"Me too!" Chloe yelled, not wanting to be left out. "I'm proudest of all!"

A few hours later, Carrie and Sam sat with Ian, Chloe, and the Jacobs twins at a long table at the Sunset Country Club. With them was Emma Cresswell, the third member of the au pair threesome, and the boys she took care of, Ethan and Wills. Carrie, Emma and Sam had become best friends the previous year when they'd met at the International Au Pair Convention in New York City. Luckily they'd all gotten jobs on Sunset Island, a fabulous resort island off the coast of Maine.

As Carrie sat at the table waiting for lunch to be served, she marveled, for the millionth time since they'd first met, that the three of them had gotten to be best friends. *We're all so different! Emma's a blonde Boston heiress;*

Sam's a tall wild redhead from the-middle-of-nowhere-Kansas; and me, well, I'm just your basic upper-middle-class girl-next-door from New Jersey. But here we are!

"You get to see Graham on TV today, Emma?" Carrie asked Emma, who per usual was wearing one of her great outfits—an all-white cotton shorts-and-top ensemble, with white matching sunglasses perched on top of her perfect blond hair.

"I sure did," Emma answered, taking a sip of ice tea. "We had it on while I was making breakfast for the kids."

"What did you think?" Carrie asked.

"I thought—"

"You thought the outfit that the last girl wore was fabulous, and you called the station right away and asked to buy it from her, and then you bought the store it came from," Sam joked.

"How did you guess?" Emma said blithely. Carrie knew that Emma was used to Sam's teasing—it hardly seemed to bother her anymore.

"Well, I thought Ian's father was cool,"

15

Ethan said. "I mean, for an old guy." He took a sip of his Coke.

"Did you see when that fat lady kissed him!" his kid brother Wills asked. "Mega-death!" He held his throat and pretended to strangle himself.

"*Eeee-yew!*" the Jacobs twins cried out in unison. "That was like the grossest thing I've ever seen," said Becky.

"Totally," Allie said.

Well, that's unusual, Carrie thought to herself with a smile. *They're actually agreeing on something.*

"Hey Ian," Becky said, fluttering her heavily mascaraed eyelashes at him, "do you think your father can get the band—*our* band—on *Donahue?*"

Carrie chuckled. The Jacobs twins had recently joined Ian's group, turning Lord Whitehead and the Zit Men into Lord Whitehead and the Zit *People*. And she knew that Ian, who looked young for his age, had a crush on Becky Jacobs, who along with her sister was quite well-developed and dangerously precocious for fourteen.

"Don't know," Ian said noncomittally. "Maybe."

"Well," Allie said, "it sure would be good for our careers."

"Uh-huh," Becky added. "I mean, any publicity is good publicity."

Carrie saw Sam roll her eyes. She and Emma started to laugh.

"I'll, uh, see what I can do," Ian said as emphatically as he could. "Let's go get something from the buffet." All the kids stood up and took their plates over to the buffet on the far wall.

"Ah, sweet silence," Sam said. The girls all laughed.

"What's your schedule for the rest of the day?" Emma asked Carrie.

"The usual," Carrie replied, taking a bite of a piece of bread. "Graham and Claudia come home tonight. Thank God. I haven't seen Billy in days. How about you?"

"Not bad," Emma said. "I have a date with Kurt tonight. He's not working for a change."

"Get down Emma!" Sam cried. Carrie smiled. For the last two summers, Emma had been involved in a major league romance with Kurt Ackerman, a very buff guy who lived year-round on the island. To help put himself through college, during the summers he worked days as the head swimming instructor at the country club and evenings as a taxi driver.

"Did you talk to Kurt about, well, you-know-what?" Carrie asked quietly. *Okay, I won't say it out loud, she thought to herself. I'm sure Emma knows I'm talking about our trip out to California, where she had a hot and heavy romance with—*

Just then a loud argument broke out by the buffet table, where an embarrassed Ethan was blaming his brother for spilling a ladle full of gravy on him in front of the ultra-cool Jacobs twins.

"My kiddies call," Emma said, throwing her napkin down and heading for the buffet.

"You didn't answer her question!" Sam called after Emma.

"Call me later, after my date," Emma called back to her friends. "I'll tell you then."

"You got it," Sam yelled. "This could be the

best gossip of the summer!" She turned to Carrie. "You think she told Kurt?"

"Honest Emma?" Carrie said. "I say she told him."

"You think?" Sam asked. "Not me. If she had told him, she'd be one sad little heiress."

"Oh, come on," Carrie said, sipping her diet Coke. "Kurt loves her. He'd forgive her."

"Carrie babe," Sam replied. "You sure do not know guys very well." Sam looked over at Emma who had managed to calm the feud between Ethan and Wills. "If Kurt Ackerman knew the truth about what Emma did, he'd drop her like a hot potato."

TWO

It was almost five-thirty that afternoon when Carrie finally unloaded Ian and Chloe, along with all their country club gear, from the Templetons' Mercedes. Ian had recently joined the club's under-15 baseball team, so in addition to the usual swimsuits, snorkels, and towel bags, he had his uniform, bat, spikes, catcher's protective gear, and mitt stashed in his duffel.

"Last one in's a rotten egg!" Ian said, as he ran madly from the car to the front door.

"No one's getting in the house without my key," Carrie said pointedly, as she helped Chloe out of her seat. Within fifteen minutes she had Chloe and Ian inside eating a pre-dinner snack and watching a movie in the

VCR while she put together a simple dinner for them.

"Carrie, you want to watch the movie with us?" Chloe came into the kitchen to ask.

"No thanks," Carrie replied, as she poured a jar of pasta sauce into a pan to heat it. "I'm kind of busy now."

"Okay," Chloe answered. "I'm going to wear my special hat while I watch," she added.

Carrie smiled to herself. *Life's pretty simple when you're four years old. Maybe my day would be a lot less nerve-wracking if I wore a special hat, too. I'll make a mental note to have a fashion consultation with Sam.*

Carrie left the sauce to simmer, then headed to the answering machine in the hall to check for messages. The red light on the machine was blinking. She flicked the *play* button and took out a pen and paper.

"You have three messages." *Beep.* "Thursday, one-forty-two P.M.," the mechanical voice said.

Beep. "Hi, Carrie, it's us," indicated Claudia's voice. "Just wanted you to know that

21

we'll be in tonight as planned, on the nine o'clock ferry. Did you guys see Graham on *Donahue* today? Hope Chloe missed the kiss. Give my love to the kids. See ya!"

Beep. "Three-fifty-six P.M. Hello, this is Zetta Hunter," said a voice with a thick British accent. "I'm with *Rock On* magazine in New York. *Rock On* is planning a story on the teen children of current pop stars, and I would like very much to speak with Ian Templeton and perhaps interview him for this story. Could Ian and one of his parents please ring me up promptly?" She gave a phone number. "Thank you!"

Carrie played the message again and double-checked the number. *Hmmmm. Interesting. I wonder what Graham and Claudia are going to think about this.*

Beep. "Five-fifteen P.M." *Just missed this last one,* thought Carrie. "Hi Carrie, it's your mother! How are you, honey! Look, Dad and I were thinking about taking off a few days and coming up to see you on your island. Maybe we'll take a day and go to Ogunquit while we're there. We'll be home tonight after seven-thirty. Give us a call. Love you! Bye."

My mother. Wow. They never take short trips. They go for three weeks on a safari in Africa, or they go on a trip to the Amazon, or . . . well, this could be fun. I'd really like Emma and Sam to meet my parents, and Graham and Claudia too. I mean, they're not bad—for parents. Carrie smiled to herself. *Don't I have practically the only mother in the world who actually approves of my boyfriend even though he has a pierced ear?*

"Hey, Carrie!" Ian's voice cascaded down the stairs and interrupted her train of thought.

"What?" Carrie responded.

"Did I hear my name on one of those messages? Was it Becky?" he asked hopefully.

"Uh, no, not exactly," Carrie said. *Oh hell,* she thought to herself. *I was going to keep that message a secret until I could tell Graham and Claudia about it.*

Ian bounded down the stairs and plopped down on the bottom step. "Well, who was it?"

"It was . . ." Carrie hesitated.

"It was a girl, right?" Ian asked. "I could hear it was a girl. What girl?"

"Right," Carrie admitted. *Okay, here goes nothing. He can't do anything about it without talking to his parents anyway.*

"So who was it?" Ian asked impatiently.

"Some girl named Zetta Hunter who's a reporter at *Rock On* magazine who wants to interview you for a story," Carrie said, as if she were reciting last week's grocery list.

Ian looked as if he had been hit in the head with a sledgehammer. Then a huge grin crossed his face. Carrie couldn't help but grin along with him, he looked so happy.

"*Yeee-ow-za!*" Ian screamed. "*Rock On* magazine! It's the biggest; it's the coolest; it's the baddest—"

"Hold on, Ian," Carrie cautioned him. "Your parents are going to have to give the okay, and you remember that *Rock On* story that Faith O'Connor did about your dad." *I don't want this kid to get his hopes up too high,* Carrie thought.

"Oh that," Ian said, a disdainful tone in his voice.

"Yes that," Carrie said. *That article last year where Faith did everything but say that your dad was completely and totally addicted to cocaine.*

"Well, that was then, this is now," Ian reasoned. "I'm sure my dad isn't going to do anything that's going to stand in the way of my career."

"Ian—"

"Excuse me, Carrie," Ian interrupted excitedly, "I've got to call the rest of the kids in the band!"

Carrie shrugged her shoulders and went into the kitchen, as Ian ran for the upstairs telephone. The pasta sauce was cooking nicely, the garlic bread was ready to bake, and Carrie turned the heat up under a big pot of water. She sat down at the kitchen table with a magazine just as the phone rang.

"Templeton residence," she said.

"Hi there," came a deep masculine voice.

"Billy!" Carrie cried with delight.

"Yeah, remember me?" he teased. "It seems like forever since I saw you."

25

"I know," Carrie replied with a sigh. "I miss you."

"Right back at ya," Billy said with a laugh. "So let's do something about it."

"Soon," Carrie promised.

"How about real soon and real private?" Billy suggested in his low, musical voice. "I had a dream about you."

Carrie felt a chill of happiness tickle its way up her spine. "What did you dream?" she asked softly.

"We were on the beach," Billy began, "and—"

Just then Carrie heard the click of the upstairs extension being picked up.

"Carrie?" said Ian. "I have to use the phone."

"I'll be off in a minute," Carrie said. She was dying to hear the rest of Billy's dream.

"It has to be now!" Ian said. "It's official band business. You know."

"Right," Carrie agreed with a sigh. "Billy?"

"Yep," Billy replied.

"Can you call me later?" Carrie asked.

"Maybe we can plan something for the weekend."

"You got it," Billy said. "Later."

Carrie hung up and went to the stove to drop the spaghetti noodles into the rapidly boiling water. But as she stared at the steam what she was seeing was herself and Billy on the beach, doing what she imagined they had been doing in his dream.

"Hello, Mom?" Carrie said, when her mother picked up the phone. "It's me!" The Templeton's dinner was over and Carrie had finally found a moment to call them. Carrie's parents had probably just gotten home from the pediatrics practice they ran together in Englewood, New Jersey.

"Oh, hi, darling! Hold on just a sec—" Carrie could hear her mother call out to her father. "Tom! It's Carrie! Come on!" Then Carrie heard her dad pick up the other extension.

"Carrie? Hi, honey!" her dad said.

Carrie smiled at hearing her dad's voice. "Hey, I got your message," Carrie said. "You

27

want to come up for the weekend? That's really great!"

"We got Dr. Thompson and his crew to cover our office through Monday night," her mother said. "So I thought we'd come up tomorrow morning. That is, if that's okay with you."

"Fine!" Carrie said. *Well, so much for a romantic weekend with Billy,* she thought for a brief second. *Okay, I'll work it in. I won't spend every waking moment with my parents anyway.*

"Great!" her father said. "I called the Sunset Inn and they've got room for us. I'll just make a reservation through Monday night. We can't wait to see you!"

"I can't wait either," Carrie said. "And you'll finally get to meet Sam and Emma— I've been telling you about them forever!"

"See you tomorrow!" her mother said. "We'll call when we get in."

Carrie and her parents said their good-byes, and Carrie hung up. She hadn't made it more than twenty feet back to the family room, where Chloe was coloring in a Disney coloring book and Ian was busy playing Nintendo, when the phone rang again.

Carrie went for it automatically. "Templeton residence, Carrie Alden speaking," she said.

"Hello, Carrie?" said a Spanish-accented voice. "It's Ray. How are you?"

"Raymond?! Wow, it's great to hear from you. What a surprise!" Carrie said happily. Raymond Saliverez had been one of her best friends in high school, as well as at Yale, where they both went to college. He was an exchange student from the small South American island of Matalan and had decided to stay on for college in America. Carrie and Ray and her high school boyfriend, Josh, used to hang out all the time. She and Ray had a platonic friendship that Carrie really valued. Ray had been planning to spend the summer back on Matalan with his family, which was why Carrie was so surprised to hear from him.

"Are you calling me from Matalan?" Carrie asked.

"No, I ended up staying in New Haven for

the summer," Ray replied. "Student services got me a summer job as a Spanish tutor."

"But I remember how much you wanted to go home for a few months," Carrie said.

"Well, I have to go back in two weeks anyway when my visa expires," Ray said.

"Yeah, that's right," Carrie said, "I remember you told me you have to get it renewed, right?"

"Right," Ray replied. But there was a strange edge to his voice.

"Ray, is everything okay?" Carrie asked.

"I thought perhaps I could come visit you this weekend," Ray said, and Carrie noticed that he didn't answer her question about whether or not everything was okay.

Carrie did some quick thinking. *My parents are coming. But they know Ray and they love him. They won't mind. I haven't seen Billy in a few days, but I can still work that in. That's no problem with Ray. There's work, but I've kicked my butt with work for the last week. Claudia and Graham will give me some extra time off.*

"I think it's a great idea!" Carrie said

quickly. "I'd love to see you—you can come and hang with me and my friends. I'd love for them to meet you. My parents are going to be here, too."

"I love Tom and Mary Beth. They were so nice to me last Christmas when I was their houseguest," Ray said. "I will stay at the Sunset Inn. I called already and made a reservation."

"Pretty confident, weren't you?" Carrie joked with him.

"Carrie Alden, you are one of my very best friends in America. I think I know you pretty well. I'll call you tomorrow after I arrive, okay?"

Carrie grinned. "Okay. Bye Ray!"

"Bye!"

Carrie shook her head as she hung up the phone and went back into the living room. *First no visitors. Then my parents. Now Ray and my parents. This is going to be an interesting weekend. But I am going to make time for me and Billy if it's the last thing I do!*

THREE

When Carrie walked into the Play Café on Sunset Island's main drag the next afternoon at twelve-thirty, she spotted Emma and Sam right away, sitting in their favorite booth under one of the café's many video monitors. Carrie had to laugh—Sam was holding a huge slice of pizza in her hands and gobbling it down while Emma neatly cut her slice into bite-size pieces.

"Hey, you two," Carrie said, as she slid into the booth next to Emma.

"We ordered already," Sam said, swallowing another bite of pizza. "Sorry, but I was starving."

"You're always starving," Carrie laughed.

"Cute outfit," Sam opined, as she looked

Carrie over. "And *très* daring for the Ivory girl, I might add."

"So glad you approve, Ms. Bridges," Carrie said with a grin. She had on a pair of golden leggings, a black tank-top undershirt, and over that a black and gold men's baseball jersey, with a pair of black Converse All-Star sneakers on her feet.

"It's really cute," Emma approved, daintily cutting up another piece of pizza.

"What I want to know is how you manage to wear white so often and never get it dirty?" Carrie asked Emma, lifting a square of pizza from Emma's plate and popping it into her mouth.

Emma had on a white cotton jumpsuit turned up at the bottom to show pink and white polka-dot cuffs. She looked down at herself and shrugged. "I think my mother drilled it into me at an early age that a lady never musses her clothes, something like that."

"Gawd, your mother would shoot me then," Sam said, dabbing at some tomato sauce that had dripped on her white T-shirt. She stood up to grab some napkins from another table, and Carrie saw that Sam had on oversized men's boxer shorts held up with Mickey Mouse suspenders, and her trademark red cowboy boots. *Only Sam could pull off an outfit like that,* Carrie thought with a smile.

"Hi ya," called Patsi, one of the waitresses. She came over and put a plate in front of Carrie. "I assumed you'd be wanting this."

"Thanks," Carrie said. "How's life?"

"Sucks," Patsi said cheerfully. "You want a drink?"

"A diet Coke, I guess," Carrie said.

"You got it," Patsi said and headed for the kitchen.

"So listen," Sam said, sipping her Coke, "I've been pressing the Boston baroness here to spill the beans on her date with Aquaman last night—as in did she tell him about you-know-who or didn't she, but I've gotten no-where so far."

Carrie gave Emma a questioning look. She was curious to know the answer to this question herself. When the three of them were out in California earlier in the summer to meet

Sam's birth mother (Sam had only recently found out she was adopted), Emma had found herself in a brief but torrid romance with Sam's half-brother Adam, a twenty-two-year-old film major at U.C.L.A. Carrie knew Emma really loved Kurt, and had been terribly confused by the whole thing. Once she left California, Emma decided that what had happened with Adam was over, but what she couldn't decide was whether or not to tell Kurt about it. Carrie remembered Sam's awful prediction—if Kurt finds out, he'll drop Emma like a hot potato. But Emma wasn't looking very upset.

"Well," Emma began, "we went out to dinner . . ."

"Emma!" Sam interrupted her. "Did you tell him or what?"

"Tell him what?" Emma asked innocently.

"About—"

"About Adam?" Emma asked. "Of course not. Why would I want to do that?"

Carrie nearly choked on her pizza. Emma, despite being able to speak five languages and having traveled all over the world, didn't consider herself very sophisticated when it came to guys. And all the way back on the plane from California to Sunset Island, she'd agonized about whether she should tell Kurt about her fling with Adam. *I was pretty much convinced she was going to come clean,* Carrie thought to herself.

"Because you said—" Carrie started to speak but Emma cut her off.

"For once," Emma said, her voice dropping to a whisper, "I decided Sam was right. Why should I tell him something that would hurt him if I know what I did was a mistake that I'll never make again?"

"Get down Emma-bo-bemma!" Sam cried. "Two guys for every girl. That's what I say."

Emma looked at Sam sharply. "This is not two guys for every girl, Sam," she said, a little irritation in her voice. "It's a question of doing the right thing for me."

"Was it weird," Carrie wondered, swallowing a piece of pizza before she spoke, "seeing Kurt and not telling him?"

Emma smiled again. "Less weird than I thought it might be. Now, isn't *that* weird? I mean, when he kissed me, it felt exactly the same," Emma spoke.

"Terminally fickle," Sam opined.

"No, it's not that at all—" Emma protested.

"Hey, guys have been getting away with it forever!" Sam interrupted. "It's our turn!"

"And speaking of guys," Carrie said, "a really terrific one is coming to visit me this weekend."

"What about Billy?" Sam asked, her eyes wide. "Whoa, this is too cool, both of you have two guys—"

"Oh, stop drooling, Sam," Carrie laughed. "This guy is a friend, period. His name is Raymond Saliverez. He was an exchange student at my high school—he's from South America. You'll love him," she predicted.

"But will Billy love him, is the question," Sam asked archly.

"Come on, Sam. I mean it!" Carrie exclaimed. "This is totally platonic! He and Josh and I used to all hang out." She told her friends all about Ray and about how he had to go back to his native Matalan in two weeks.

As she got into the story, Emma got a far-away look in her eyes.

"I've been to Matalan," Emma said. "On holiday with my parents, years ago."

"Figures," Sam grunted.

"It's one of the most beautiful places in the world," Emma told them. "But the government—not so great. They just recently got democracy."

"I know that," Carrie said. "Ray and his family are very politically active—they worked hard for the change."

"So, you're absolutely sure this thing with Ray is just buddy-to-buddy?" Sam asked.

"Absolutely," Carrie said.

"Good, then maybe I'll give Pres a run for his money," Sam decided. "Is Ray cute?"

"You are incorrigible!" Carrie shrieked.

"Just a joke, just a joke," Sam assured her.

"I've got more news," Carrie told them. "My parents are coming here this weekend, too."

"You have parents?" Sam joked. "Why haven't we met these humans?" she demanded.

"Because these humans share a busy pediatric medicine practice in New Jersey and it's hard for them to get away," Carrie answered.

"So, does this wreck your weekend?" Emma asked.

"No, I actually like my parents," Carrie said.

"I can't imagine what that's like," Emma said archly.

"They're sweet," Carrie said, knowing how lucky she was. Emma's parents were divorced and she wasn't close to either of them, and Sam was still going through a weird thing with her parents because they hadn't told her that she was adopted—she had accidentally found out.

"Sweet parents—I can't imagine it," Emma said wistfully.

"They're very political, too," Carrie continued. "Seriously liberal democrats."

"Old hippies?" Sam asked hopefully. "Do they smoke dope and sit around singing 'We Shall Overcome'?"

"Not exactly," Carrie laughed. "They give a lot of money to political causes, work with an anti-nuclear power group, that kind of thing."

"I think that's great," Emma said. "I mean,

my mother thinks that politics is like rotten fish—best to stay away from."

A wolf-whistle cut through the clatter of the Play Café. The girls turned their heads to the door. Walking toward them were Billy and Pres.

"Hey, we don't respond to that kind of sexist hog-call," Sam said, teasing the guys.

"Speak for yourself," Carrie said. She knew Billy was only joking. *I am so happy to see him!* she thought to herself, and jumped up and into his arms.

Billy kissed her. Sam and Emma and Pres all applauded. Carrie grinned sheepishly, and then she and Billy slid back into the booth.

"If that's the kind of greeting I get when you don't see me for a few days," Billy joked, "maybe you need to work harder."

"No thanks," Carrie said with a laugh. She couldn't stop grinning. She was just so happy to see him!

"So, what's up?" Pres asked in his slow Tennessee drawl. He twirled a curl of Sam's hair around his finger.

"Carrie's got visitors coming this weekend," Sam told him. "Her parents. And her friend Ray from South America."

Carrie explained to Pres who Ray was and how she knew him. She'd already told Billy about him.

"Hey, that's cool that he's coming," Billy offered. "I've wanted to meet him; he sounds really interesting."

"This Ray is from Matalan?" Pres asked, a look of worry flitting across his handsome features.

"Yeah," said Carrie. "What's wrong?"

"Well," Pres said, drumming his fingers nervously on the table as he spoke, "I may be wrong about this, but I think I saw a report on CNN this morning that said there was a coup d'état there last night. The army's now in control."

"Coup d'état?" Sam asked. "What's that?"

"It's French," Emma explained quickly, "for blow against the state. Or more specifically, 'overthrow of the government.'"

Carrie felt her heart beating rapidly. *Ray's family is really politically involved there,* she thought. *His father was a big activist for the democracy movement. If there's been a military takeover, they could be in real trouble—Oh my God. His visa expires soon. Ray's got to go back there! I've got to find out more!*

Carrie stood up. "Patsi!" she called to the waitress. "Can we turn on the TV? It's important!"

"Sorry," Patsi called back. "It's broken. The repair guy said he'd be here already, but—"

Carrie didn't wait to hear the rest. She grabbed her purse. "Excuse me," she told her friends. "I've got to get to a TV." She bolted from the Play Café, leaving her friends behind looking after her in astonishment.

Carrie drove the Templetons' Mercedes as fast as the law would allow. She raced through their front door, and switched on "Headline News" on cable television. Within a couple of minutes, there was a report on the coup in Matalan. Carrie watched the report, and then breathed a sigh of relief.

The report said that while overnight it had

appeared that rebel army units had taken control of the government, the latest report was that pro-democracy forces had regained power and that the president was still in control.

Thank God, Carrie thought. *I never thought I'd care so much about what's happening on an island off the coast of Venezuela.*

Carrie was watching the rest of the news when Ian's voice in heated argument with Graham and Claudia spilled into the living room.

"But Dad," Ian was saying, "this interview could be the most important day of my life!"

"I don't care," Carrie heard Graham say, "There is no way I am letting *Rock On* interview you. Case closed." Graham, Claudia, and Ian appeared in the doorway of the living room.

"Hi, Carrie," Claudia said. "As you can see, we've got a little problem here."

"Little problem?!" Ian exploded. "The biggest music magazine in the world wants to interview me about my band and my stupid parents say no. I'd say that's a big problem."

Oops, Carrie thought. *Family argument. Time for me to make myself scarce.* She stood up and started toward her room.

"Carrie, don't go," Claudia said quickly. "You did some work for *Rock On,* right?" Carrie nodded. She'd taken photographs for the story that Faith O'Connor did about Graham, and Faith had tried to force her to take every damning shot of Graham she could possibly take.

"So why don't you tell Ian what I'm afraid of?" Graham said. "Maybe he'll listen to you. He's obviously not listening to me." Graham's voice trailed off. *He may be the biggest rock star in the world,* Carrie thought, *but right now he's just an ordinary father having an ordinary fight with his kid.*

"I think your dad is afraid that the press often says it's going to write one thing, and then writes something very different," Carrie said slowly. She wasn't very comfortable in the role of explaining adults to Ian.

"Yeah, well, that's about grown-ups like you," Ian said. "They don't do that to kids. And I'm a kid."

Grown-ups like me? Carrie thought. *I'm a grown-up?* "How do you know that, Ian?" Graham said. "You saw what Faith O'Connor tried to do to me. They're vultures." He fidgeted uncomfortably in his seat.

"Dad, Faith O'Connor's not writing this article!" Ian retorted. "Why are you standing in the way of my career?"

Bull's-eye! Carrie thought. *Graham probably doesn't think much of Ian's industrial music band, but he's certainly not going to do anything that will allow Ian to blame his band's failure on him.*

"You're still young," Claudia said gently. "You have plenty of time." She looked affectionately at her son.

Ian glared at her. "The opportunity is now, Mom," he said earnestly. "You always tell me to strike when the iron is hot. Well, right now the iron is on fire."

Carrie saw Graham roll his eyes. "Okay Ian," Graham said, "let me suggest a compromise."

"What?" Ian asked sullenly.

"I'll give the okay to *Rock On* to do the story

45

because I agree that it'll be good for your band," Graham said.

"So what's the catch?" Ian asked dubiously.

"I want them to use Carrie as the photographer on the story," Graham concluded, shooting a look at Carrie. "That is, if it's okay with your mother and with Carrie. I don't want one of their hack photographers making you look bad."

Me as photographer? Carrie thought. *That means another photo credit in* Rock On. *Yeah, but it's a photo credit for shooting the Zit People. Okay, I can't be choosey.*

Ian looked hopefully at Carrie. "Car, will you do it?" he asked, his voice full of expectation.

"Sure Ian," Carrie said, "if *Rock On* agrees."

"Okay, Claudia?" Claudia nodded. "Okay, son?" Graham looked at Ian, whose scowling face had been transformed into a grin.

"Okay, Dad," Ian said. "And thanks."

"I hope I'm not making a mistake," Graham said to Claudia.

"I'm gonna be in *Rock On*." Ian sang, getting up out of his chair and dancing around the room. "I'm gonna be a rock star! I always knew it would happen!"

Carrie exchanged a look with Graham and Claudia, and once again it felt odd to be in the role of "adult," worrying about a kid.

Oh, what am I worrying about, Carrie thought, getting up from the couch. *Everything is okay in Matalan, Billy loves me, and Ian's happy.*

She skipped up the stairs, singing one of Graham's songs.

And I'm gonna be shooting pictures for Rock On *again,* Carrie thought. *I hope this experience with them is an improvement over the last. Although, it couldn't get any worse.*

FOUR

"Sam, move Ian a little to the left. That's better," Carrie said, as she fiddled with the focus mechanism on the camera slung around her neck.

It was later that same day, and Ian had the Zits assembled in the soundproofed basement so that Carrie could take some sample photographs for the article.

Now, if only these kids would stay still! Carrie thought. *They're so excited they're going to be in* Rock On *that they're practically leaping around the room. Fortunately, I've got Sam as my stylist. Unfortunately, the Jacobs twins are now part of this band.*

"Ian, I don't think it's fair," Becky whined, as she and Allie posed in front of a mirror in their official Lord Whitehead and the Zit People regalia—yellow rain slickers with various types of refuse Super Glued on at random—pop tops, cotton balls, old newspapers, etc.

"What's not fair?" Ian said, basking in the attention from Carrie and Sam. Carrie snapped off a few sample shots and then moved some of the lighting instruments around.

"It's not fair that you should be the only one interviewed," Allie piped up. "It's sexist."

"Yeah," Becky agreed, as Sam re-glued some Day-Glo plastic sunglasses that were missing a lens to her raincoat.

"When you start your own band and you get as successful as I am, then you can get interviewed," Ian told her, brushing some hair out of his eyes.

"Gag me with a spoon," Allie muttered.

"Guys," Carrie said, gesturing to the three other guys who made up the original Zit People, "can you get behind your instruments so I can take a group portrait? Ian in front." The three boys scrambled for their places behind the various hulked-out appliances and industrial equipment that made up Lord Whitehead and the Zit People's arsenal of instruments.

"Sam, fix Ian's hair," Carrie added. Sam quickly moved to comb one of Ian's locks down over his forehead. "Great, that's it." Carrie snapped off a few more shots.

"Okay, that's a wrap," she announced.

"Wrap what?" Marcus Woods, one of the band members, asked.

"I mean I'm done for now," Carrie translated. She unslung her camera from around her neck and started to take down her tripod.

"We're done?" the Jacobs twins crooned in unison.

"We're not done, Carrie," Ian explained, as if Carrie had gotten stupid in the last five minutes. "The band has to practice the tunes we're going to play for Zetta at the interview."

"Ah, gee Ian, I don't think you have to actually play for her," Carrie said. *God forbid Zetta actually hears the Zits,* Carrie thought with a shudder.

Sam snorted back a laugh and Ian shot her a killer look.

"Of course, we're going to play for her," Ian told Carrie. "Why else would she be coming?"

This time Sam spoke up. "Because she's doing a story on the kids of rock stars and—"

"Oh, come on Sam," Becky said. "She's coming because she's heard how great we are."

"Yeah," said Allie. "We're a lot hotter than the Flirts, you know," she added superciliously.

The Flirts, or Flirting With Danger, was Billy and Pres's rock band. Sam, Emma, and their archenemy, Diana De Witt, sang back-up for them. The Flirts were very well-known in the New England area, and hoped to get a recording contract soon.

"Much hotter," Becky agreed smugly. "Who's gonna be in *Rock On* first, us or you?"

"Oh come on," Sam began.

"Oh come on nothing," Ian interrupted. "I say we practice our number for *Rock On*. Places everyone!" All the kids ran for their spots.

"This is one of our best," Ian whispered to Carrie confidentially. "One . . . two . . . one . . . two . . . three . . . four," Ian counted off. He reached for the play button of a nearby cassette player, and the voice of some folk singer Carrie didn't recognize filled the basement studio:

Michael row your boat ashore, hallelujah
Michael row your boat ashore, hallelujah
Michael row your boat ashore, hallelujah
Michael row your boat ashore, hallelujah

As the singer reached the second "hallelujah," the Zit People all joined in on their appliances, beating them mercilessly with iron pipes. Ian sang along with the tape, and the Jacobs twins sang the line "I'm a-gonna row it," over and over again.

Thankfully, the song ended quickly. When it was over, the kids looked at Carrie and Sam expectantly.

"So," Ian said, "what did you think?"

Carrie looked at Sam before she answered. Sam looked like she would rather be anywhere else than in the basement with the Zit People at that moment.

"Well," Carrie said, "it is original."

"We're the next wave of rock and roll," Ian said proudly. "The whole country's gonna know about us soon." He turned back to his band members and called them together for a quick conference.

Carrie turned to Sam. "The next wave of rock and roll . . ."

Sam laughed. "That's true," she quipped. "And when that wave crashes, rock and roll may never be the same again."

"Mom, Dad," Carrie looked at her parents, who were approaching the long table that Rubie—Kurt Ackerman's adopted aunt—had set up for their group at her restaurant, Rubie's Diner, "I'm so glad to see you!"

It was the next evening, and Carrie's parents had arrived a couple of hours earlier. Ray came just an hour before them, and had met up with Carrie at the Templeton's house. Carrie had made a reservation at Rubie's Diner, and arranged to meet her parents there. Kurt and Emma had come along, too. Unfortunately, Sam had to work.

"Oh, sweetie, you look great," Carrie's mom said, giving her a huge hug.

"You too!" Carrie said, hugging both her parents.

"You look just like your mom!" Emma exclaimed.

"Everyone says that," Carrie said with a laugh. "Let me introduce everybody. This is Emma Cresswell—" Carrie began.

"We've heard a lot about you!" Carrie's father broke in jovially. Emma blushed happily.

"And this is Kurt Ackerman, Emma's boyfriend," Carrie continued. "You know my buddy Ray, and these are my parents, Mary Beth and Tom Alden," Carrie finished.

"Ray," Mary Beth said, grinning. "It's good to see you. And you can come back to our place for Christmas anytime if you'll make that fabulous fish stew again." Ray grinned back. Carrie remembered how he had insisted on doing the cooking one night when he was visiting the Aldens for Christmas. He had whipped up a Matalan seafood stew that was the best stew any of them had ever tasted.

"Sit, sit!" Rubie called from across the restaurant. "I'm preparing a special feast for you!"

"This food will be outrageous," Kurt predicted, taking a seat at the table.

Carrie smiled happily at Ray and her parents. It was so good to see them! Ray grinned at her, and she was reminded of how handsome he was—on the short side, but slim and muscular, with deep, golden skin, huge brown eyes and incredibly long eyelashes.

"I'm bringing over wine for a toast," Miss Rubie warned.

Kurt laughed. "Rubie's sentimental—she loves a good family reunion."

"Me too," Carrie's mom said, squeezing Carrie's hand softly.

"So, do you like the Sunset Inn?" Emma asked Carrie's parents.

Carrie's dad launched into a funny story about a couple with four dogs in designer doggie outfits, who kept parading the dogs around the lobby, and Carrie's thoughts drifted away.

What a whirlwind, Carrie thought. *First a big date with Billy last night after the photo session with the Zits, then Ray and my parents arrive. Too bad Sam isn't here, and Billy had band practice tonight—*

"Carrie?" Emma got Carrie's attention. "I know Sam had to stay with the twins, but where's Billy?"

"He had some band business in Lewiston today—he's taking a demo tape to WBLM radio for some new band show they're putting together. And then he had practice."

"He's a nice young man," Tom said, smiling at his daughter. Carrie smiled back.

Rubie edged up to their table and put down an ice bucket with a bottle of sparkling cider in it. "On the house," she told them.

"Rubie, you're a sweetheart," Kurt said, getting up to give her a hug.

"Number one guy on the island!" Rubie said.

"I agree!" Emma said, looking right at Kurt. They all laughed heartily.

"You ain't never gonna forget this dinner," Rubie predicted. "Hope you're all hungry!"

"Totally awesome!" Ray exclaimed, in a perfect accent-free imitation of a twelve-year-old American kid.

"Hey, that's hilarious!" Kurt exclaimed. "How'd your English get so good?"

"It's not so great," Ray said, self-effacingly, and he looked at Kurt with his dark eyes.

"Are you kidding?" Kurt asked. "You speak better than a lot of Americans!"

"Well, I have been in the United States for most of three years now," Ray said. "Also, my father insisted that my brothers and I study languages from the time we were five. I speak French, too."

"Really," Kurt said. "Here in the United States, most kids have trouble enough with English."

"You don't know how good you have it," Ray said, shaking his head. "This is a wonderful country. Stable. You all heard about what is happening in Matalan?"

Everyone nodded. The attempted coup in

Matalan had gotten a little story in that morning's *Portland Press-Herald.*

"It is a tragedy," Ray said. "We are such a small nation, and we are still fighting each other."

"Your country's only been a democracy for a few years, right?" Tom asked.

Ray nodded. "Yes. And we fought hard—"

"Okay, enough politics!" Rubie's voice boomed out in the dining room. "Open your bubbly and drink a toast or something!"

Kurt obliged, pouring some cider into everyone's glass.

"To friends and family," Carrie said, lifting her glass.

"Here, here!" Her father agreed, and everyone clinked glasses, then took a sip of the cool drink.

"Time to eat!" Rubie called, and carried over an enormous tray laden with steamed mussels and clams, broiled lobsters, corn on the cob, and bottles of Coca-Cola. She laid the tray down in the middle of the table.

"I'm giving the orders here now," she said, in a stern voice. "Now, dig in!" They all laughed, filled their plates, and started eating.

"Ray, what are you talking about?" Carrie said, trying to remain as calm as possible at what her friend was telling her over the phone.

It was around eleven-thirty that night, and Carrie had been surprised to hear the phone ring. She figured it was some musician buddy of Graham's, but Claudia answered and yelled upstairs that it was for her.

"Carrie, I'm not kidding!" Ray said, his voice cracking with emotion.

"But that's impossible! I mean, the newspaper reported this morning that—"

"The newspaper was wrong!" Ray interrupted her. Carrie could hear that he was almost in tears. "There's been another coup attempt and this time they succeeded. The army is running my country now!"

That is completely impossible, Carrie thought. *I mean, I spent this afternoon at the beach hanging out with my friends. How could the government of Matalan have been overthrown while we were swimming in the ocean?*

"Who told you this?" Carrie asked sharply. She found she was biting her cuticles as she spoke. "How'd you find out?"

"My father. He called me at the Inn fifteen minutes ago—and the phone cut off in the middle!" Ray's voice was filled with agitation. "He said the army had closed the airport and that he couldn't get out!"

"Oh God," Carrie breathed into the phone. She knew how politically active Ray's parents were. They were virulently opposed to this regime, and were well-known in Matalan. His parents could be arrested, even killed! Ray had told her too much about the harsh reality of Matalan's politics for her to be naive about the gravity of the situation now. And then a frightening thought dawned on Carrie.

"Ray?" she whispered, clutching the phone hard. "You're not going to have to go back there when your visa expires, are you?"

Carrie could actually hear him crying. "I don't know," he said softly, "I don't know.

Maybe your government will give me political asylum."

"But what if they don't?" Carrie cried.

"If they don't" Ray said, with a catch in his voice, "then I could be a dead man."

FIVE

Carrie's eyes were focused on Chloe Templeton, as she splashed about in the kiddie pool at the Sunset Country Club. But her thoughts were far away in Matalan. *I just can't believe that Ray's going to have to go back there! I've got to think of some way he can stay here. They'll kill him!*

It was the next morning, and Carrie felt exhausted and anxious as she stared at the shimmering pool. It was all she could do to keep an eye on Chloe—her thoughts kept drifting back to a terrible nightmare she'd had the night before, when she'd finally drifted off to sleep.

It was the worst dream of my entire life, she thought. *Ray was on trial in Matalan, but he didn't understand anything that the judge or the jury was saying. Then, they dressed him in white robes and led him out in front of a firing squad of about a thousand soldiers with rifles. One soldier gave the word, and the others fired at him. And then I woke up, drenched in sweat, so scared . . .*

"Hey girlfriend!" Carrie heard Sam's voice as she and Emma walked into the pool area of the club. Carrie mumbled a hello.

"What's wrong, Carrie?" Emma asked, a worried note in her voice. "You look like you just saw a ghost. Have you been crying?" She and Sam sat down on a couple of wicker chairs across the round table from Carrie. They pulled their chairs closer to hers.

Carrie took a deep breath and tried to compose herself, but could feel warm tears roll down her face.

"It's Ray," she said, choking the words out. "Something terrible has happened." She managed to tell the whole story to Sam and Emma, but found herself in tears again at the end. Sam reached into her purse and pulled out a package of tissues, which Carrie took gratefully. She blew her nose and tried to compose herself.

"Have you talked to your parents about this?" Emma asked. "You said they were pretty politically active. Do they have connections? Maybe they could do something."

"No," Carrie said, "I haven't. They left for Ogunquit early this morning and they're not coming back to the island until late tonight."

Sam shook her head. "I find this hard to believe," she said finally. "You mean the United States would just send Ray back there to fend for himself?"

Emma nodded. "You can only stay in a foreign country if you have a visa. Most of the time, that is."

"So what if he were to stay here anyway?" Sam asked.

"He'd be an illegal alien," Carrie explained. "And then they'd just kick him out as soon as he got caught."

"So he'd be, like a fugitive or something?" Sam asked.

Carrie shook her head. "It's not like in a spy

movie, Sam," she explained. "Believe me, Ray has no place he can run."

"But we can't send him back if it means he's going to be killed!" Sam said. "That's just not right!"

Carrie glanced over at Chloe to make sure she was okay. She was splashing around in the kiddie pool with a couple of playmates.

"Ray told me last night there's a chance that he might be given political asylum in the United States," Carrie said gravely. "But it's not a sure thing."

"Oh come on," Sam chided. "Of course the United States will give him asylum! This is the land of the free and the home of the brave, and all that stuff!"

"Ha," Carrie said flatly.

"What do you mean, 'ha?'" Sam shot back. "No way is America sending a guy like Ray back if he could be in danger—"

"Sam, there are thousands and thousands of people trying to get political asylum in the United States!" Carrie yelled, taking her anger and upset out on her friend. "Look at all the Haitians! Look at all the Asians! Look at all the Africans! Do you really think our government is going to bend over backwards for a college student from Matalan?!"

Sam looked at Carrie contritely. "Look, I'm no expert on international relations, I just thought—"

"It's okay," Carrie sighed. "Sorry I yelled. It's just that I feel so helpless."

Emma bit her lip pensively for a moment. "Well, actually Carrie, there is one thing you could do to guarantee that Ray could stay in America. But I don't think you'll be too enthusiastic about the idea."

"What's that?" Carrie asked skeptically. *As if I haven't already thought of every possible thing,* she said to herself.

"You could . . . well, you could marry him," Emma said simply.

"I could *what*?" Carrie asked, sitting up and looking at her friend.

"Marry him," Emma said again. "You're an American citizen, so if he married you, he could get his green card."

"Hey, I saw some movie with a plot like

that!" Sam exclaimed. "This French guy wants to stay in the United States, so he gets this American girl he hardly knows to marry him, so he can get his green card. But then they go for a meeting with the government and . . ." Sam's voice trailed off.

"And what?" Carrie asked, anxious to learn everything she could about this subject.

"And the government kicks him out anyway because they can tell it wasn't a real marriage," Sam continued sheepishly. "The two of them didn't know enough about each other, so they failed his immigration interview."

But Ray and I are great friends; we know everything about each other; we've talked about everything, Carrie thought rapidly to herself. *I know the name of his mother and father and brothers, even what his favorite flavor of ice cream is.* And then Carrie stopped herself. *Wait a sec. I am not marrying Raymond Saliverez. I have a boyfriend. I have a life!*

"Forget it," Carrie said emphatically. "I can't do something like that."

"Of course not," Emma replied. "It was just an idea."

"I don't think it's such a terrible idea," Sam said, slipping her sunglasses up on top of her head.

Carrie and Emma stared at her.

"Don't look at me like I grew horns!" Sam exlaimed. "I just meant it's not like you'd have to stay married to him and bear his children or something. You'd just have to stay married to him for a while."

"But . . . but that's nuts!" Carrie cried.

"I don't know," Sam said with a shrug. "If I needed to do something really, really big to save your life, or Emma's life, I'd do it. That's all I'm saying."

Carrie and Emma looked at Sam in astonishment. *Sam, the one who doesn't care about politics, is actually in favor of me doing this?* Carrie wondered.

"Sorry," Carrie finally said. "I love Ray, and I'll help him any other way I can, but I can't marry him. That's final."

"Not as final as it will be if he gets sent back there," Sam said softly.

"If you're so gung-ho on it," Carrie said, getting more upset as she spoke, "why don't you marry him?"

"I could," Sam said, matter-of-factly. "But we'd never pass the test. He's not *my* old friend."

When Carrie walked into the Play Café a few hours later to meet Ray for lunch, as they had planned the evening before, he was already sitting in a booth and reading the *New York Times*. Ray saw Carrie come in; he stood up and greeted her warmly.

"Ray," Carrie said quietly, "I'm so worried. How can you be smiling?"

"It is better to be here with you than it would be to be at home," he said simply. "Here, I am safe. There, who knows?" He shrugged his shoulders.

Carrie sat down in the booth. "Have you tried to call your family today?" she asked, barely glancing at the menu.

"Yes," Ray said. "Somehow my father got through again. He and my mother and my brother are already in a safe house—it would

69

be very dangerous for them to stay at home. He says that the army has announced that it will stay in power for two years and then hold elections."

"That's some consolation!" Carrie said trying to be optimistic.

"That's—how do you say it here?—the oldest line in the book," Ray replied, matter-of-factly. "My father thinks that as soon as he shows his face again, he'll be arrested. Look, I'm hungry," he continued. "Can we eat?"

Patsi overheard Ray, and stopped by to take their order. Carrie, who didn't feel much like eating, ordered a small salad and a glass of iced tea. Ray ordered a club sandwich and a glass of orange juice. They purposely talked about everything but politics until their food arrived.

"Look, Ray," Carrie said, toying with her salad, "my friend Emma told me that if you were to arrange a green-card marriage, you could stay in America no matter what."

Ray took a bite out of his sandwich. "Your friend Emma is very smart," Ray said, "but it is not so simple. The INS is getting very strict."

"INS?" Carrie asked.

"The Immigration and Naturalization Service of your government," Ray said. "They are very strict now, and they make sure that a couple is really married in every sense of the word. If a couple doesn't pass the test, the immigrant is deported right away."

"You knew about green-card marriages!" Carrie said, incredulously. "Why didn't you say anything to me about it last night?"

Ray took another bite out of his sandwich. "It was not for me to bring it up," he said simply. "You are one of my best friends—I would not ask you to do that. I hope I can find another way."

"Is there another way?" Carrie asked, hopefully.

"Depends," Ray said. "The best would be political asylum. Or maybe the INS will make a special exception for me. That is possible. Or maybe I will become an illegal."

"You can't do that!" Carrie said.

"There are millions already in America doing it," Ray said, "many of whom speak Spanish like me. What do you think? Do you think I would make a good dishwasher?" He turned and flexed his arms like a body-builder. "I am strong!" he laughed.

"Ray, why are you joking?" Carrie asked. "This is serious!"

Ray looked in Carrie's eyes before he answered. "I am laughing because I am afraid that otherwise I will cry," he said. There wasn't a glint of a grin anywhere on his face as he said it.

Carrie got an idea. *What about Jane and Jeff Hewitt? They're both lawyers, and they helped Kurt Ackerman when he was falsely arrested. Maybe they can help Ray!*

"Did you know that the people Emma works for are lawyers?" Carrie asked Ray. She was excited by her own thought.

"No, but—"

"Maybe they can help us!" Carrie said. "They're really smart, and really nice."

"But I don't want you to—"

"Don't be silly, Ray," Carrie stood up as she finished her sentence. "I'll be right back."

Carrie went over to the phone, dialed the Hewitts, and had a brief conversation. She came back to the table smiling the first smile she had managed all day.

"It's on," she said. "No ifs, ands, or buts, Ray. I'm picking you up tonight at seven and taking you to see them."

"But what about your parents?" Ray asked. "Aren't you—"

"My parents aren't getting back 'til late," Carrie said. "And they'll agree that this is more important." Carrie knew she wasn't just saying that. *They really will think this is more important,* Carrie told herself. *What's more important than a matter of life and death?*

When Carrie and Ray walked into the Hewitts' living room that evening, Jane and Jeff Hewitt and Emma were waiting for them. They stood up to greet Ray, and Jeff said a few words to him in Spanish. Jane guided Carrie and Ray to two empty seats on a couch.

"Everything okay with you?" Jane asked Carrie.

"Besides this, everything's fine." Carrie answered. "Ian's going to be in *Rock On* magazine—they're coming to interview him tomorrow afternoon."

"That should be interesting," Jeff said with a grin. Even he had heard about the antics of the infamous Zit People.

Jane got everyone cold drinks, and then she and Jeff turned their attention to Ray.

"Carrie filled me in on your problem," Jeff said to Ray, "and I took the liberty of calling a friend of mine in Boston who specializes in this kind of thing."

"And?" Carrie interrupted eagerly. "What did he say?"

"Do you know about green-card marriages?" Jeff asked Ray.

That subject again, Carrie thought. Her heart sank. *There must be some other way!*

Ray nodded.

"If the INS doesn't give you political asylum, that's probably your best chance," Jeff said. "But it's highly illegal and there would be many complications. As a lawyer I would not recommend it, but I can advise you if that's what you choose."

Ray nodded again.

"The fact that the new regime is saying they'll eventually hold elections makes it a lot less likely that you'll be granted political asylum," Jane said.

"But the elections aren't really going to happen!" Carrie cried, remembering what Ray had told her.

Jeff Hewitt stretched his legs. "Maybe not," Jeff said. "But basically, the U.S. looks for any reason they can, *not* to give people refugee status."

Carrie looked at Ray. He was still nodding. *He knows all this,* Carrie thought.

"So what should Ray do?" Carrie asked, insistently.

"Wait until Monday," Jane said, "when the Federal Government gets back in business. I'll make a few phone calls for him then."

"And what about until then?" Carrie said, wringing her hands together unconsciously.

"My suggestion," Jeff said, his eyes grave, "is to pray."

SIX

"Carrie, it's for you!" Claudia called up to Carrie. She was busy helping Chloe into her bathing suit for her swim lesson. "Don't forget that Chloe's due at the club in a half hour!"

"I know," Carrie called back, heading for the phone.

"And don't forget that Ian's got to be back here for his interview at two o'clock!" Claudia added. "If he misses it, he'll never speak to you again."

Carrie didn't even manage a small smile. *It's so absurd,* she thought. *Chloe's going to her swimming lesson; Ian's going to be in a magazine, and I'm shooting pictures; but in three weeks, my best friend could be lined up*

77

in front of a firing squad. It's just so damn unfair!

"Hello?" Carrie said, picking up the hall phone.

"Hi, Car, it's me," came Emma's warm voice over the phone. "How are you?"

"I've been better," Carrie admitted.

"I can't find my red sneakers!" Chloe yelled to Carrie.

"Just a minute!" Carrie yelled back.

"Didn't mean to interrupt," Emma said quickly. "I just . . . I don't know. I felt so awful after you and Ray left last night. When Jeff told us to just pray I got the most terrible feeling of dread."

"That's how I'm feeling twenty-four hours a day," Carrie said. "It doesn't seem real!"

"I know," Emma commiserated. "Listen, if there's anything I can do . . ."

"Thanks Em," Carrie said. "I wish there were."

"I don't know how to say this exactly," Emma began slowly, "but if perhaps money would help . . . "

Carrie smiled for the first time that day. "I

wish. This may be one time that money won't change anything, but thanks for offering."

"I guess it was a silly idea," Emma admitted. "I thought maybe someone could be bribed or something."

"Well, if so, I sure don't know who or how to do it," Carrie said sadly. "If I did, I'd do it. I wouldn't care if it was illegal. Some things are bigger than laws."

Carrie thought back to the late-night phone conversation she and Ray had had after their meeting with the Hewitts. Ray hadn't been able to sleep and he had called her in desperation. After talking through all of his other options and realizing their futility, he had broken down and actually asked Carrie to marry him! He said he hadn't wanted to put her in that position but it was starting to seem that there was no other way for him to stay out of danger.

"And after all," he had added, trying to muster some of his usual good humor, "if you do end up marrying me, I want to at least be on the record as having proposed like a gentleman."

Carrie could not forget the fear and desperation she'd heard in his voice, and she wanted more than anything to help him through this.

But what will this do to my life? And to me and Billy? she thought, feeling her own fears rise inside her. She quickly pushed them aside in disgust, telling herself, *Forget about your own stupid problems. Ray's life is on the line. And now that the cards are on the table, you better get yourself together and figure out how you're going to play your hand!*

"So the thing is," Becky Jacobs bragged to a group of kids as she spread tanning oil on her legs, "*Rock On* is sending its top young writer to interview us. That means it's gonna be a really, really big story."

"That girl is so full of it," Sam murmured to Carrie. "No wonder her eyes are brown."

Carrie kicked Sam's leg, but other than that she didn't move. It was an hour later, and Carrie was lying on a chaise lounge near the pool, hoping that some inspiration about Ray's predicament would dawn on her. Instead of being able to concentrate on Mata-

Ian, however, she was being treated to the loud voices of Becky, Allie, and Ian bragging about their imminent "fame."

"Wow," one of the younger girls breathed. "You must be so excited!"

"Sure," Becky shrugged casually, as if such an interview was an everyday occurrence.

"I love your bathing suit," another girl told Allie with reverence.

"It's okay," Allie said, fixing the band on her skimpy red bikini.

"I see fame means even your bathing suit gets famous," Sam whispered to Carrie.

"I'll be doing the talking for the interview, of course," Ian piped up, irritated that the twins were stealing his thunder. He was sporting a new pair of jet-black wraparound sunglasses and baggy black swim trunks, playing up his image as a rock star.

"I'm spending the whole morning laying on my back," Allie announced, lifting her face to the sun. "I need the extra color for the photos." She looked over at Carrie meaningfully, "And they better be good!"

"Such sweet girls, aren't they?" Sam asked sarcastically.

"Life is so weird," Carrie mused. "One minute you can be carefree and the next minute your life can be in danger."

"The monsters' lives are always in danger," Sam said darkly. "I threaten to kill them on a regular basis."

"You know what I mean," Carrie said. "It's hard right now for me to care much about photographs and interviews in magazines." She told Sam about the meeting with Jane and Jeff the night before. "Even they sounded pretty hopeless about the whole thing," Carrie finished. *And even they talked about a green-card marriage,* she added to herself. *But I can't do it! I just can't!*

"Hi, you two," Emma said, walking over to Sam and Carrie. She glanced over at Becky, Allie, and Ian before she sat down on a chaise lounge. "I see that the threesome is holding court."

"The main thing," Ian said, running his hands self-consciously through his hair, "is that this could be the big breakthrough that industrial music needs."

"You're right," one boy said, hanging on Ian's every word as if it were the Gospel According to Ian.

"It's only a matter of time," Allie said, stretching her legs languorously, "before we get the really big dates, like with Johnny Angel."

"Johnny Angel!" one girl screeched. "He is so awesome!"

This even got Carrie's attention. She and Emma both looked at Sam. Sam had had a fling with none other than the rock star Johnny Angel on a yacht the summer before.

"Can you imagine if the twins knew about you and you-know-who?" Emma teased.

"They'd never believe it," Sam stated flatly. "They think I'm over-the-hill—like Johnny Angel would never look at a girl over fifteen."

Even Carrie smiled at that.

"You have that 'my-mind-is-working-overtime' look on your face," Emma told Carrie, pulling her sunglasses out of her beach bag.

"It is," Carrie admitted. "Not that it's getting me anywhere."

"Did you think anymore about what we talked about yesterday?" Sam asked. "About marrying him?"

Carrie sighed. "Yeah," she admitted, "I've thought more about it." *Actually, when you get right down to it, I haven't really thought about anything else. Who am I kidding?*

"What have you been thinking?" Emma said gently.

Carrie was silent for a minute. *What have I been thinking? That's a good question. I've been thinking that if I don't marry Ray I'm the most rotten person on the face of the earth, and I've been thinking that if I do marry him I'm the stupidest, and I'm giving up my whole life for some guy, which is exactly what I never ever wanted to do.*

"I'm totally confused," Carrie said, finally.

Suddenly, the group of kids around Ian and the twins burst out in hysterical laughter at some remark Allie had made.

Carrie felt like crying. *Life is just so unfair,* she thought bitterly. *That group of kids over*

*there, all excited about the Zit People inter-
view with* Rock On, *has absolutely no idea of
the turmoil that I'm in, or that Raymond
Saliverez is in the biggest trouble of his life—
and if they knew, they'd barely care.*

"Maybe if you lay out the issues one by one
it would be clearer for you," Emma suggested.
"We're not going to tell you what to do."

Sam nodded in agreement at Emma's suggestion. She even raised her right hand in the
Girl Scout pledge position. "Even I, Sam
Bridges, Advisor to the Stars, do solemnly
swear to keep my mouth mostly shut while
you talk," she pledged.

Carrie smiled. *I am so lucky to have them as
my friends,* she thought.

"But first," Sam added, "I've got to tell you
that it's nice to be listening to your problems
for a change, instead of telling you all of
mine."

"I second that!" Emma said quickly. The
girls all laughed again.

"Okay," Carrie said. "The more I think
about the whole thing, the more I think I
have to at least consider marrying Ray—"

"Wow, does that sound strange!" Sam interrupted, then she clapped her hand over her mouth. "Sorry," she added.

"I know I said I wouldn't do it, and I'm not saying I will," Carrie added quickly, "but I'm . . . thinking. You see, Ray called me late last night. He couldn't sleep and seemed really desperate. He actually asked me to marry him, though he said he hadn't wanted to put me in that position. But he was so desperate. . . ."

"Go on," Emma urged.

"Well," Carrie said, taking a deep breath. "It's just that . . . well, first thing, I have a boyfriend. I really like Ray, but just as a friend—okay, a very, very good friend. But what will marrying him—even if it's a marriage only in name—do to my relationship with Billy?"

"You've got a point," Emma said.

"But you can still see Billy," Sam said, "Ray will understand completely."

"But it's not as easy as that," Carrie said. "If we get married, the INS is going to come visit us, and interview us. Ray and I will have to get an apartment. We'll have to live together, know absolutely everything about each other. . . ."

"Everything?" Sam asked pointedly.

"You mean would I have to sleep with him?" Carrie asked, alarmed.

"If I meant 'sleep' I wouldn't be worried," Sam replied wryly.

"Okay, you mean would I have to have sex with him," Carrie qualified. "No. Uh-uh. Absolutely not."

Emma and Sam stared at her.

"At least I don't think so," Carrie added in a small voice.

"No, of course you wouldn't have to do that," Emma assured her. "The INS can't be that thorough when they question you!"

"Right," Carrie said firmly, as if she were trying to convince herself. "First of all, I wouldn't do it, and second of all, there's only so understanding I can expect Billy to be!"

"This would be really hard on your relationship with him," Emma said.

"She could still see Billy," Sam told Emma. "He'd still be her boyfriend."

"How do you think Pres would like it, Sam," Carrie asked pointedly, "if you and he were really serious, and he came to visit you during the winter, and you were living in a one-bedroom apartment with some guy he barely knows, but who you say is your best friend, and who Pres knows is your husband? How do you think that would be?"

"It's not really my idea of marriage," Emma said, readjusting her chair to better catch the late morning sun.

"Well, it's not anybody's idea of a marriage," Carrie said bitterly. "I know it's sort of uncool, but I've always dreamt about having a really traditional wedding—me in a long white dress—and friends like you two as my bridesmaids. It's what I've always wanted."

All three of them were silent for a moment.

"You should have that one day," Emma finally said.

"Well, maybe you and Ray wouldn't have to stay married for years and years," Sam offered. "Things are bound to calm down in Matalan sometime. Maybe later on you could have that big, romantic wedding with Mr. Right."

"It wouldn't be the same then," Carrie said with a sad sigh.

"Maybe not," Sam agreed. "But sometimes you gotta do what you gotta do!"

"What does *that* mean?" Carrie said, turning to her.

"It means that life isn't fair," Sam said, scratching a mosquito bite on her shin.

That's what I've been feeling all day long, Carrie thought.

"I mean, is it fair that Emma here should be rich and I should be poor," Sam continued, "when I would obviously enjoy being rich so much more than she does? No, it is not!" All three girls grinned a little at Sam's joke.

"I just don't want to do anything that I'll completely regret later," Carrie said earnestly.

"You won't know that 'til later, will you?" Sam asked rhetorically.

"No, I guess I won't," Carrie answered. "But I sure wish I could know how things will turn out."

*   *   *

"So Ian . . ." Zetta Hunter made a few notes on a reporter's pad as she spoke in her British accent, "could you give me some idea—some insight, if you will—of what it's like to be Graham Perry's son?"

Carrie watched closely, checking out angles around the basement studio, and she snapped off a few pictures as Ian formulated his response. Ian and the band were sitting on the steps of the Templetons' basement, with Ian on the lowest step and the rest of the Zit People occupying the upper steps. Zetta was standing at the bottom of the steps conducting the interview.

"It's made music the most important part of my life," Ian said, looking to his band for confirmation. They all nodded their heads. "The most important part of all our lives."

"Interesting," Zetta said, smoothing out some imaginary wrinkles in the short, black leather miniskirt she was wearing, and adjusting the input controls on her small cassette recorder. "Then your father is the inspiration for your music?"

"Oh no!" Ian said quickly. "Industrial music is the response of Lord Whitehead and the Zit People to an over-industrialized, over-polluted world. Our inspiration's over-complication." Ian grinned.

In that moment, all of Ian's silly pretentiousness fell away and Carrie saw the sweet kid she knew and loved. She quickly snapped a picture.

"Really," Zetta marveled. "How innovative. Do you think I might be able to hear a number or two? If it wouldn't be any trouble?" She smiled an ingratiating smile at Ian and ran her hand through her spiky black hair.

She looks like what I'd think a British rock and roll writer should look like, Carrie thought. *Super-hip clothes, pale skin, red lipstick, spiky black post-punk haircut, fab earrings . . .*

"Sure thing!" Becky Jacobs piped up. Ian whirled around and gave her a look that could kill a small animal.

"I'll do the talking for the band," he stage-whispered at her. "So shut up."

He turned his attention back to the *Rock*

On reporter. "We'd be delighted," he said brightly. "Places everyone!"

Oh God, Carrie thought. *This is going to be a musical nightmare.*

And then Lord Whitehead and the Zit People whipped through perhaps the worst version of "Michael Row Your Boat Ashore" that Carrie had ever heard. Done the Zit People way, of course. Carrie forced herself to snap action pictures all the way through. Then she turned and looked at Zetta Hunter.

Unbelievable. She's smiling.

"Innovative!" Zetta said with enthusiasm. "Ground-breaking! Ground-breaking, indeed!"

"You mean you really liked it?" Ian asked incredulously.

"Liked it?" Zetta said. "I loved it! Sort of reminds one of the Sex Pistols when they were starting out, only angrier."

"Wow," said one of the guys in the band. "I think—"

"Sssssh!" Ian said.

Zetta gathered her notebook, cassette recorder, and the rest of her things. "I don't usually say this," she said, "but I can practically guarantee that the story about you will appear in Tuesday's issue."

"Awesome!" Ian exclaimed, then remembered to act cool. "I mean, that would be okay," he added lamely.

"And I can practically guarantee this," Zetta said, her voice dropping nearly to a whisper. "Your life afterward will never be the same."

SEVEN

"I vaguely remember you," Billy was saying teasingly into the phone. "You're the real cute brunette, curvy, smart, all that?"

"Oh, Billy," Carrie sighed into the phone. It was later that night, and Carrie was midway through dressing for dinner with her parents when Billy called.

"So look, I know you've got this big dinner planned with the folks," Billy said, "and Ray's here and all, but maybe we could get together later?"

"I'd love to," Carrie said softly.

"How about I meet you on the beach, by the far pier at, say eleven?" Billy suggested.

"You got it," Carrie agreed. "I'll be the cute brunette—watch for me."

"I'll be the cute guy missing the cute brunette," Billy said huskily before he hung up.

Carrie walked back into her room and sat on her bed, staring at the wall. *I can't marry Ray,* she thought miserably. *I can't. I love Billy and it would ruin everything.* "I wish somebody could tell me what to do!" she wailed out loud.

But there was no answer, except the loud beating of her own heart.

Carrie was stunned when at dinner that night her parents raised the question of the trouble in Matalan and what it meant for Ray. The black-and-white-dressed waitress at the Sea Grotto (a new place that had just opened on Main Street), had just brought them steaming bowls of clam chowder which Carrie didn't feel much like eating. She looked over at Ray, who hadn't even picked up his spoon. Evidently he didn't feel like eating, either.

"I understand there are a lot of problems back home for you Ray," Carrie's father said.

"We've been following it on the news pretty closely."

"Yes sir," Ray said politely. "It is not a very big story for most Americans but it is a very big story for Raymond Saliverez and his family." He smiled a little.

"Have you decided what you are going to do?" Mary Beth Alden asked, dipping her spoon into her clam chowder.

Okay, Carrie thought. *I've never been coy or had to beat around the bush with my parents, and I'm not going to start now.*

"This is a big problem for Ray," Carrie said before he could answer. "His visa expires in just a couple of weeks."

Carrie's father nodded his understanding. "I'll say it's a big problem. You don't want to go back there now, do you?" he said.

Ray shook his head. "I think it would be a mistake—maybe a fatal mistake," he said.

"I understand," Tom said. "You know, during the Vietnam War we had some friends go to Sweden rather than stay here, because they were afraid that the government would send them to Vietnam to fight. I think this is much worse."

"It is much worse," Carrie said. "Ray could be killed! Isn't there something you could do?"

Carrie's dad looked at his wife. "We could call Congresswoman Leonard," he said. "Maybe she could help."

"That's an idea," Carrie's mother agreed. "We'll do that when we get home."

"Thanks, Mom," Carrie said, turning to Ray. "My parents are very active in the Democratic Party, and Leonard is a Democrat."

The waitress came, took away the soup bowls, and placed a small salad in front of each of them. Carrie stared at the lettuce. She had never felt less like eating.

"Unfortunately, there's no guarantee that Anne Leonard can help," Tom said. "I'm not sure that the State Department is going to pay any attention to our Congresswoman."

"I spoke with the people Emma works for— the Hewitts, right?" Ray asked, looking at Carrie for confirmation. She nodded. "They are lawyers and they are going to make some inquiries for me on Monday."

"Good," Mary Beth said, brightening. "You have to think of every possibility."

Okay, Carrie thought, as her mother turned her attention to the salad in front of her. *She said it, not me; she said the words "every possibility."*

"Mom, Dad?" Carrie began softly, trying to keep herself from trembling. "What do you think about green-card marriages?"

Her parents looked uneasy.

"I mean, in unusual circumstances," she continued quickly.

Carrie's dad took a sip of water and nodded seriously. "We were wondering whether Ray had thought of that. It's not easy to do these days."

"That's what we've read, anyway," Carrie's mom agreed. She turned to Ray. "Still, if you can find the right girl, and make the right arrange—"

Carrie took a deep breath and interrupted her mother. "I meant with me, Mom. A green-card marriage with me."

Conversation at the table stopped. Mr. and

Mrs. Alden looked at one another. They were speechless.

It never occurred to them it could be me, Carrie realized.

Carrie's mother spoke first. "Is this something you've given much thought to?"

Only every waking moment, Carrie thought to herself miserably. "I've been thinking about it a lot," Carrie said quietly. "I'm not saying Ray and I have decided to do this," she added quickly. "I just wanted your opinion."

"But Carrie," her father finally spoke. "You're only nineteen—"

"I know how old I am, Dad," Carrie said in a low voice.

Her father shot a look at Ray. "Surely you understand that we'd hesitate to see Carrie get involved in this—"

"Of course," Ray said with dignity.

"But what if it would save Ray's *life*?" Carrie demanded.

"Perhaps Ray could go underground," her mother ventured.

"You mean be an illegal alien?" Carrie asked harshly. "And do what, wash dishes in some dive, spend every waking moment hiding, worrying that someone will turn him in? Is that what you want?"

"No, no, Carrie please," her father said earnestly, putting his hand on his daughter's arm. "We're just trying to explore solutions here."

"I have told Carrie that I think it is too much to ask of her," Ray said in a low voice.

"Oh Ray, this is no time to be polite!" Carrie exploded. "You could be polite and dead!"

No one at the table spoke.

"Carrie, you're not a child," her mother finally said. "You have to make your own decision. There's nothing we can do to stop you."

Now, what the hell does that mean? Carrie asked herself. *Nothing we can do to stop you? Does that mean that if you do it you're on your own?*

Tom quickly swallowed the salad he'd been chewing, and looked at his daughter. "I guess I have to agree with your mother," he said. "Carrie, you can get in a lot of trouble if you get caught—both of you," he added, looking over at Ray. "There are a lot of issues involved here."

Tears came to Carrie's eyes. *So much for my parents the great liberals,* she thought miserably. *Real liberal when it comes to everyone else, not so liberal when it comes to me. Not that I've made up my mind, but it would have meant so much to me if they'd support me, no matter what. . . .*

"Look, it's not that I've definitely decided to get married," Carrie said, working to keep her voice even. "I just wanted your input because Ray and I are thinking about it as an option."

Carrie's mother pressed her lips together and looked at her daughter sadly. "I've told you what I think, sweetie," she said gently. "I don't know what else to tell you."

"Dad?" Carrie asked.

"It's a very big decision, Carrie, getting married," he answered, "for whatever purpose. Don't take it lightly."

"Believe me, I don't," Carrie said firmly.

"Maybe we can think of someone better for Ray to marry!" Mary Beth said hopefully.

"Now, there's an idea!" Carrie's father agreed.

Carrie stared sadly at her parents. *I know they're doing this because they love me,* she reminded herself. *And I know I'm not even sure myself what to do. But just at this moment I wish they'd love me a little less, and stand by the principles they taught me a little more.*

After saying good-bye to her parents and to Ray, Carrie headed for the far pier, even though it was only ten-thirty and she wasn't supposed to meet Billy until eleven. She needed some time alone to think.

There was a chill in the air, and Carrie pulled the sweater she'd brought with her closer around her. She stared out at the endless, fog-clouded sea. *It's so huge,* Carrie thought, *and no matter what happens with us little humans, the sea just keeps on going. There is so much in this world that is bigger than I am. . . .*

"Carrie!" a pleasant female voice called over the wind.

"Carrie Alden!" a second voice, a little higher pitched, reached her. Carrie peered through the evening mist to see who was trying to get her attention. Back on the boardwalk she could just make out the forms of a girl in a wheelchair and another tall, athletically built young woman standing next to her.

Darcy Laken and Molly Mason! Now what are they doing out here at this time of night? Carrie wondered.

Emma, Sam, and Carrie had befriended Maine-native Darcy the summer before, when Emma was doing some door-to-door fund raising. She had visited the strange-looking house on the hill where Molly lived with her parents. Molly had been injured in a car accident, which put her in a wheelchair permanently, and Darcy was hired by the Masons as Molly's live-in assistant. Carrie couldn't think of a person better suited for the job. Tall, strong, and resourceful, Carrie had liked Darcy right from the start. Darcy also had psychic ability and sometimes had dreams or "flashes" about events before they happened. *Right now I can use all the help I can get.* Carrie thought remembering Darcy's gift. *Paranormal or otherwise.*

"Hi!" Carrie said walking up to Darcy and Molly and plopping herself down on a bench. "What brings you two out here at this hour?"

"It's our favorite time," Molly said. "No one to stare at me in my wheelchair." Carrie knew that Molly, a former equestrian, was embarrassed that she now was a wheelchair-bound paraplegic.

"Don't mind her," Darcy said, in her normal matter-of-fact tone, "it's Feel-Sorry-for-Molly Night. We have them once a week or so."

To Carrie's surprise, Molly laughed. "You see what I put up with?" she asked Carrie.

"So, what's up?" Darcy asked, sitting down next to Carrie. "Were you thinking great thoughts out there on the beach?"

And though Carrie had absolutely no intention of telling Darcy and Molly what was going on with Ray Saliverez, she suddenly felt as if a dam had broken inside her. The whole story poured out.

"So the thing is," Carrie finally concluded, "I still haven't decided what to do."

"Wow," Darcy exclaimed.

"Double-wow," Molly agreed. "That's a tough one."

Darcy nodded. "Molly's right. It's not like there's any one right answer, you know?"

"But maybe there is," Carrie said earnestly, staring down at her clenched hands. "I mean, I can't let Ray just go back there if there's something I can do to prevent it!"

"You said his family is in hiding," Molly reminded her. "Maybe he could go into hiding with them."

Carrie shook her head. "They'd get him at the airport in Matalan, as soon as he got off the plane," she said morosely. "And they'd take him to jail. He's on a list—that's what his father was able to find out."

"Horrible," Molly commiserated. "Really horrible."

"I know it's probably silly," Carrie said to Darcy, pushing some wind-blown hair behind her ear. "But I guess I was hoping you might have some kind of . . . flash about this."

"You mean a psychic flash," Darcy said with a sigh. "I wish I did, Carrie, honest. I wish I could help you. The awful thing is, I have no control over this stupid psychic stuff."

"She means it just happens sometimes," Molly translated.

"Right," Darcy agreed. "Whenever I really want to know something, I don't know anything! And then half the time when I do know something, the images are so strange that I'm not sure how to interpret them!"

"Ah, the curse of the working-class psychic," Molly teased.

"Oh well," Carrie said with a sad shrug. "It was worth a try."

"Sorry I'm not more help," Darcy said. "I can give you an opinion, if you want."

"She's *exceedingly* opinionated," Molly put in.

Darcy nudged Molly playfully. "Seriously," she said. "I think you need to follow your heart."

"But my heart doesn't know—" Carrie began.

"Yoooo-hooooo! Here comes the bride! Here comes the bride!" Darcy, Carrie, and Molly all stopped talking and turned their attention down the boardwalk, where two people were singing at the top of their lungs.

"Oh God, I'd recognize those voices anywhere," Carrie groaned, putting her head in her hands.

"Here comes the bride. Here comes the bride," chanted the singers. Finally, they came into view—it was none other than Diana De Witt and Lorell Courtland, the two girls Carrie loathed most in the world.

For reasons Carrie had never been able to fathom, Diana and Lorell had been hateful to her and her friends from the moment they had met. Diana had even managed to seduce Kurt the summer before—and he and Emma had broken up over it for a long time. Carrie stared morosely as Lorell and Diana sauntered over to them.

"Well, if it isn't the Bride of Frankenstein," Lorell cooed in her soft Georgia twang, as she looked right at Carrie.

"Yes indeed," Diana agreed with relish.

"How hot is his Spanish blood—everyone on the island wants to know!"

Carrie felt her face turn red. *What are they talking about, the entire island? How did everyone—*

"Why Carrie, how sweet!" Lorell trilled. "You're actually blushing! You can't expect to carry on your affairs in public and then expect no one to find out, can you?"

"I got a look at the guy," Diana added in a confidential voice. "He really is hot. But then, I hear Latin guys are the hottest."

"Just go away," Carrie said in a tired voice.

"How inhospitable!" Lorell said with indignation.

"Go far away," Carrie added. "I'm in no mood to enter into your juvenile banter, okay?"

"Well, I for one am simply cut to the quick!" Lorell cried.

"Oh, me too," Diana said in a lazy, nasty voice.

Darcy stood up slowly to her full height of five foot ten. Not a willowy five foot ten. A powerful five foot ten.

"Girls," Darcy said cheerfully, "you're boring us. So you've got exactly five seconds to turn around and walk the other way. Or else I'll pound the crap out of you. One at a time. Who'd like to be first?"

"My, my," Lorell said, "threats are so tacky!" But she turned around and started to walk the other way, and Diana followed.

"Thanks for that," Carrie said gratefully.

"Nice going!" Molly said to Darcy. "You're such a bruiser," she teased.

"I just can't stand them," Darcy said. "And I refuse to waste my time." She turned to Molly. "I'm getting cold. You ready to boogie?"

"If I could boogie, stupid, I wouldn't be in this chair," Molly answered.

Darcy laughed. "Bye," she told Carrie. "Hope you work out your problems."

"Let us know what happens with Ray," Molly added with a wave, and the two of them headed off down the boardwalk.

"What's supposed to happen with Ray?" a male voice asked. Carrie turned around, and there was Billy, smiling at her.

"Oh God, I missed you so much!" Carrie cried, throwing herself into his arms.

"Carrie," Billy whispered huskily, and kissed her until the stars swam in the sky.

"I really love you," Carrie whispered to him, tears in her eyes.

"Hey!" Billy objected with a laugh. "Love is nothing to cry about!"

"I know," Carrie said fiercely, burying her face in his warm, familiar smelling neck.

Billy held her at arms length and gave her a puzzled look. "Are you okay?"

"I'm fine," Carrie lied. *I can't talk to him about Ray. I just can't!* she thought miserably. *I don't want to do anything to ruin the time we have together.*

"Are you sure?" Billy asked.

"Just kiss me," Carrie insisted, wrapping her arms around his neck.

He did. And for a while, Carrie didn't have to think at all.

EIGHT

"Sam, this is Ray Saliverez. Ray—Sam Bridges," Carrie introduced her two friends. It was early the next morning at the Sunnyside, a tiny place on the Boardwalk that was open for breakfast. Sam had called Carrie at seven A.M.—an unheard of time for Sam to even be awake—and told Carrie she wanted to have breakfast with her.

"Early," Sam had said, "before the monsters get up and I have to become their slave."

Since Carrie had already arranged to have breakfast with Ray, she invited Sam to come along.

"I'm pleased to meet you," Ray told Sam, taking a seat at the small table. "I've heard a lot about you."

"Lies, all lies," Sam said breezily, sipping a glass of orange juice.

"Sam, I can't believe you beat us here," Carrie marveled. Sam was always late.

Sam shrugged and pushed some of her red curls out of her face impatiently. "I really wanted to talk to you," she said.

Carrie was taken aback. This was a serious Sam, one she rarely saw. "So talk," she said simply.

"Not before coffee!" Sam said, aghast.

Carrie laughed. "Ah, that's the Sam I know and love."

The waitress poured three cups of steaming coffee and took the breakfast orders. Then Carrie patiently waited while Sam poured tons of milk and sugar into her cup.

Sam took a long sip, "Ahhhh," she sighed. "Much better."

Ray laughed. "If you ever had really good South American coffee, you would not put all that stuff in it," he predicted.

"Oh, yes I would," Sam said seriously. She stared at Ray for a moment. "Listen, I wanted to talk with Carrie about what's going on with the two of you. I guess I can do that with both of you, huh?"

"If you are Carrie's friend, you are my friend," Ray said simply.

"Cool," Sam agreed. "So listen. I could not sleep last night. I just kept thinking about this big mess of yours—no offense, Ray," she added quickly.

"No problem," Ray said easily, sipping his black coffee.

"I know I said I wouldn't give you any advice," Sam continued, looking earnestly at Carrie. "Well, the thing is—I lied."

Carrie couldn't help laughing. "Go ahead," she said with a sigh.

"Now tell me again exactly what the situation is," Sam demanded. "I want to make sure I haven't forgotten anything."

Carrie and Ray rehashed the events of the last few days and Sam listened attentively.

"Who has the eggs over easy?" the waitress asked, carrying over a tray of food.

"I do," Carrie said.

"Cheese omlette?"

"For me," Ray said.

"Strawberry waffles, double order of bacon, side of hash browns and the toasted bagel must belong to you," the waitress said, putting it all down in front of Sam and then hustling off.

"You have a healthy appetite," Ray remarked with amusement.

"I can't think on an empty stomach," Sam replied, digging into the waffles. "Mmm, not bad." She wiped off her mouth and took a slug of orange juice. "Look, Car, I know you and Emma think I'm, like, this frivolous person," Sam began.

"We don't think that!" Carrie interrupted.

"Yeah, sure," Sam snorted. "I know I'm not an intellectual like you, and I don't speak five languages like Emma, but . . . I feel things, you know?"

"I know you do," Carrie said. "And you don't need to put yourself down."

"Oh, I'm not," Sam said blithely. "I pretty much have zero interest in all that stuff. I guess what I'm trying to say is that just because I'm not an intellectual doesn't mean that I'm dumb. Hey, could I try your toast?" she added to Carrie, grabbing a piece.

"Cut to the chase, Sam," Carrie said. "Ray and I have to be at the Hewitts' in an hour."

"Okay," Sam agreed, actually looking up from the food. "I think you guys should get married."

Carrie was silent for a moment. "Well, that's cutting to the chase, all right."

"I thought about it a lot," Sam added.

"It's funny," Carrie mused. "I would have guessed that Emma would have told me to do it, and you would have told me not to do it."

"I know," Sam agreed. "But, hey, I'm a complex babe!"

Ray laughed out loud. "You are very charming and very funny, too. But this is something Carrie must decide for herself."

"Absolutely," Sam agreed. "And I'm with you either way, girlfriend," she added to Carrie fervently. "But you know me. I couldn't just keep my mouth shut."

"Well, I got the idea that you were leaning in this direction before," Carrie said wryly.

"Yeah, I guess you did," Sam agreed. "But

last night what really hit me was how often people say they love each other, you know? But then when push comes to shove, all it is is stupid words."

"Yeah, I know," Carrie said softly, looking at Ray. She knew Sam was right. And she knew that the proverbial push might just be coming to the proverbial shove.

"Try not to be nervous," Carrie told Ray as they walked into the Hewitts' house an hour later.

"I'll try," he said.

Jane and Jeff had made some phone calls on his behalf to the INS in Boston, and had managed to arrange for a phone appointment with an immigration officer.

"Good morning," Jane greeted them pleasantly. "Let's go into the office."

She ushered them into a comfortable room filled with law books, a desktop computer and printer, and a speaker phone.

"Sit anywhere," Jeff said, moving the morning paper off the leather couch.

Ray and Carrie sat nervously on the couch.

"I'll place the call," Jane explained, "and I'll act as Ray's lawyer. That means he can talk, and I can talk, but not you. Okay Carrie?"

Carrie nodded to show she understood.

"Don't be surprised if you don't get direct answers now," Jeff added. "Bureaucrats don't like to move fast."

"I'm going to let you do most of the talking," Ray said. "I think these guys prefer to deal with lawyers instead of foreigners."

"You think right," Jane said, getting out a yellow legal pad and placing it on her lap. "Everyone ready?"

Everyone nodded. Carrie grabbed Ray's hand and gave it an encouraging squeeze. He smiled at her gratefully.

Jane dialed the INS number, and they all listened as the switchboard transferred the call to a number of offices before finally reaching Agent McCarthy.

"McCarthy here," answered a stern female voice.

"This is Jane Hewitt on Sunset Island, Maine," Jane said. "I think you were expecting my call."

"Right," McCarthy said, without a trace of warmth in her voice.

"It's about Raymond Saliverez, the Matalan national. My associate in Boston arranged this conference," Jane said, sounding very professional.

Carrie was impressed: Jane sounded so self-assured. *Please God, let this help Ray,* Carrie prayed.

"So?" McCarthy said impatiently.

Jane shot a quick look at Jeff as if to say, "This is not getting off to a good start."

"As you know, Agent McCarthy, Mr. Saliverez's student visa expires in a matter of days," Jane said, speaking distinctly. "There has been a coup d'état in his country."

"I'm aware of that," McCarthy said.

Jane rolled her eyes. Carrie felt herself start to perspire.

"Mr. Saliverez has a well-founded fear of persecution if he returns to Matalan." Jane said. "His family has actively supported democracy for their country, and therefore, he wants to apply for political refugee status."

"Refugee status, huh?" McCarthy barked a

short laugh. "Let me read something to you." Carrie heard the sound of papers being shuffled in McCarthy's office.

"Here it is," McCarthy continued. "Just circulated by fax."

"What is it?" Jane asked her.

McCarthy cleared her throat. "State Department Report Number 38749-21-12. On the situation in Matalan. It says that the United States State Department has formulated no position on the coup on the island nation of Matalan, but takes note with interest that the coup leaders have promised to hold elections in two years and to work for the reestablishment of democracy."

Carrie saw Ray frown and shake his head in disgust as McCarthy read the document.

"So basically—" Jane started to speak, but McCarthy cut her off.

"So basically it means that we're not considering requests for political asylum from Matalan at this time," McCarthy said curtly. "Too bad your client's not from China!" Carrie heard McCarthy laugh at her own lame joke.

Jane was silent for a moment. She looked

at Ray, who shrugged his shoulders sadly. Then she turned back to the speaker phone.

"Thank you, Agent McCarthy," Jane said.

"Thank you, Counselor," McCarthy said. "Now, is there anything else?"

Jane said no. McCarthy hung up on her end. Carrie, Ray, Jane, and Jeff sat quietly in the Hewitts' home office.

Strike-out, Carrie thought. *That got us exactly nowhere.*

Finally, Ray spoke up. "Well, that was pretty much what I expected," he said. "Look, is it okay if I try to call my father from here? Maybe he will have some information that will help us."

"Sure Ray," Jane said solicitously.

Ray moved to the telephone and dialed the number his father had given him. "I'll tell my father that I'm with you and then we'll switch to English," Ray said. "He speaks English very well."

Carrie and the Hewitts nodded assent.

"Hola? Diga." came a male voice in Spanish on the other end of the phone.

"Buenos días, Juan. Soy Ray. Está Papá?"

Carrie, who'd taken four years of Spanish, mentally translated that Ray was asking his brother Juan if their father was at home.

In rapid Spanish, Ray's brother told him that their father had been hoping to speak with him, and he quickly put their father on the phone.

"Papá," Ray said, and told his father about the situation in Spanish. He then suggested that they switch to English.

"Ray, I beg of you, you must not come here. It is very bad," Mr. Saliverez said in his accented English.

"Papá, these two lawyers here are working very hard for me, but I don't know if they can do it," Ray said with his voice full of emotion.

"Ray, I did not want to tell you this," Mr. Saliverez said.

"What Papá? *Dígame*." Ray said.

"The army, *el ejército*, they were here this morning," Mr. Saliverez said.

"Oh Papá!" Ray cried. "They found the safe house?"

"There was—how do you say it—a tip-off," Ray's father said. "We were able to hide, but now we must move to another location. It is no longer safe here."

"Where will you go?" Ray asked, clutching the phone desperately.

"I cannot say on the phone," Mr. Saliverez said. "But I will reach you soon, my son."

"But, Papá—" Ray began desperately.

"Hijo, en el nombre de Jesus, do not come back!" Mr. Saliverez implored his son. "Do whatever you must. Do anything to stay in the United States. Anything!"

"But Papá—"

Carrie, Ray, Jane, and Jeff heard a high-pitched noise from the phone. The connection had been cut off. Tears coursed down Carrie's cheeks as Ray quickly tried to redial the number. The call would not go through.

"Damn," he said.

"I think we should call Agent McCarthy at the INS and tell her what just happened," Jane said, swallowing her own emotion so that she could try to help Ray. She went over to the phone and redialed the INS. As before, the call snaked it's way through the

INS bureaucracy before Agent McCarthy answered the phone.

"Agent McCarthy," came the brisk voice.

"Agent McCarthy, this is Jane Hewitt again—the lawyer in Maine. We just spoke about the young man from Matalan," Jane said.

"And I said we aren't taking any applications for political asylum," the woman said. "I thought I was clear."

"But we've just talked with Mr. Saliverez's father in Matalan and—"

Agent McCarthy cut Jane off. "I'm sorry, but our policy on this is clear," she said. "Mr. Saliverez's father can contact the American consulate in Ciudád Matalan."

"No, that's not possible!" Jane said firmly. "The situation there is more dire than you people seem to realize—"

"Look, Counselor. I don't set policy," McCarthy said. "They'll have to go through the proper channels. Now please excuse me."

Carrie heard the phone click off.

"Well, isn't she a lovely person," Jeff said sarcastically.

"I think I must go to Boston," Ray said, standing up. "Perhaps if I see them in person . . ."

Jane Hewitt stood up. "I don't think it is going to do much good, Ray," she said.

"I don't think I have much choice," Ray replied, looking at the clock. "It is now eleven o'clock. I could be at the INS in three hours."

"But Ray!" Carrie said. "Jane said—"

"How much do you charge per hour, Jane," Ray asked. "I mean when you are doing lawyer work?"

"I bill at $175 an hour," Jane replied, "but—"

"You're hired," Ray retorted. "Starting now."

"So the thing is, Billy, Ray is in terrible danger," Carrie finished sadly. She leaned back against the bleachers they were sitting on and studied Billy's profile.

It was later that afternoon. Carrie and Billy were in the stands at a baseball field in the only public park on Sunset Island. Carrie knew it wasn't the most romantic setting, but she had to chaperone Ian, who was playing in a game there. She had invited Billy to come the night before. And although she had just told him about the horrible danger Ray was in, she was not going to discuss the possibility of a green-card marriage—no matter what—she was afraid to face what it might do to their relationship.

"The poor guy," Billy empathized. "I really feel badly for Ray."

"The situation is horrible," Carrie said. "The INS isn't going to do anything. Neither is the State Department."

"Yeah, well, America picks and chooses where to shed her benevolence," Billy said sourly. "Meaning Matalan probably has no economic advantages to offer the United States."

Carrie sighed and stared out at the carefree kids playing baseball. "You really believe that?" Carrie asked. "It's so cynical."

"Oh, come on, Carrie," Billy chided. "You're not that naive."

"No, I'm not," Carrie agreed with a sigh. "I just never had to face it myself before."

"Yeah," Billy agreed. "It sucks." He watched a chubby kid strike out. "Hey, wait a minute, what about one of those green-card marriages?" Billy asked eagerly.

Carrie felt her heart take a quick jump into her mouth.

"What about them?" Carrie asked carefully. *Oh God, I don't want to talk about this!* she thought to herself desperately.

"Maybe we can find someone for him to marry!" Billy exclaimed.

"Maybe," Carrie said in the same careful voice. "Like who?"

"Well, I don't know," Billy said. "What about someone who needs the bucks or something? I'm sure Ray would be willing to pay someone if it meant he could stay in the United States."

"It doesn't work that way," Carrie explained. "It used to be that someone like Ray could marry a total stranger, but times have changed."

"Changed how?" Billy asked.

"Now the INS checks really closely when an alien marries an American," she said. "The two people have to really live like husband and wife—they check everything out scrupulously."

"And if the couple doesn't check out?" Billy asked.

"Then the person is immediately deported," Carrie sighed. "Ray would be better off trying to lose himself in New York or something than to face that."

"So, you're saying that if Ray were to marry, he'd have to marry someone who knows him really, really well," Billy said darkly.

Carrie stared straight at him. "That's right," she said quietly.

Billy stared back at her. "You mean you, don't you."

Carrie was silent for a moment. Down on the field, some kid had just smacked a double to left-center, and the other kids and their parents were jumping up and down and yelling for him to run. Carrie, however, was oblivious to that.

"Yes," she finally said.

Billy ran his hand over his face. "Carrie . . ."

"What?"

"I . . . I don't know what to say," Billy muttered.

She took his hand. "I haven't said I'm doing it," she reminded him. "I'm just thinking about it."

"It really, really stinks," Billy finally said.

"I know, it's not fair," Carrie agreed. "I mean the coup is ruining innocent people's lives, and—"

"I'm not talking about the coup," Billy said, his voice getting tight and emotionless. "I think it stinks that you think you have to personally save the world."

Carrie sucked in her breath hard. "No, it's not that, Billy. It's just—"

"Look Carrie," Billy said, his voice dropping to a whisper as people around them started to notice the serious conversation they were having. "You and I are just beginning to really get to know each other. I care about you a lot. Hell, I love you!"

"And I love you!" Carrie put in quickly. "That wouldn't change!"

"Bull!" Billy snorted. "You don't believe that!"

"I do!" Carrie protested.

"Carrie!" Billy cried. "You'd be married to another guy!"

"But not really—" Carrie began.

"What, you're not going to sleep with him?" Billy demanded. "Is that what you mean?"

"Of course not!" Carrie cried. "How could you even think that?"

"Oh hell, Carrie, I don't know what to think," Billy groaned.

For a moment they were both silent. The sounds from the baseball game filled the air. *How can I make Billy understand?* Carrie thought. *Especially if I don't understand, myself. And what if he doesn't? I can't lose him! I just can't!*

"Billy, don't you see?" Carrie said softly. "This is a matter of life and death. I really need you to understand."

"It sounds as if you've already made up your mind," Billy said bitterly.

"I haven't," Carrie assured him. "But I have to know how you feel." *Please understand,* she prayed silently, staring at his handsome face and the sun glinting off the small stud in his ear. *Please.*

"How I feel . . ." Billy began. He turned and stared at her hard. "Carrie, I care about you a lot, more than my music sometimes, but the fact is that I'm not going to get myself—us—into a really complicated mess. It would never work."

"But it would!" Carrie protested.

"And I care about Ray," Billy continued, "whether you believe me or not. He's your friend. I'll help you do anything reasonable—I'll bust my ass to help you. But please, please, don't marry him if you want you and I to go on together."

Carrie continued to sit silently. Ian came up to bat, but she didn't see him. She stared straight ahead, tears falling silently down her cheeks.

I've never been more confused or mixed up in my life. And nobody can help me, she thought. *Nobody.*

NINE

"Carrie," Mary Beth Alden said to her daughter over the telephone. "I promise we'll do everything we can for Ray."

"Thanks Mom," Carrie said. She rubbed her eyes tiredly, and tried to push back the feelings of anger toward her parents. They had been welling up ever since the dinner three days earlier when she'd brought up the possibility of her green-card marriage. In spite of everything that was going on, she had seen her parents several times, and were calling from their hotel to say good-bye—they were about to leave for New Jersey—and nothing was settled.

"We mean it, Carrie," her mother said.

"This isn't just something we're giving lip service to."

"Well, what about me doing everything I can for Ray, then," Carrie asked.

Her mother was silent. "I just don't want you to do anything foolish," she finally said.

"Mom, it seems like a double standard to me," Carrie said flatly. "One standard of right and wrong for your daughter, and a different standard for the rest of the world. You said you had friends who had green-card marriages and you supported them. Why is it different for me?"

"Maybe you'll understand when you have a daughter yourself," her mother said softly.

"You mean 'if,' not 'when'," Carrie replied with irritation. She regretted the words as soon as they popped out of her mouth.

"I'll put your dad on," her mother said.

"Carrie, don't take your confusion out on your mother," her dad said when he got on the phone.

The anger flared again, setting Carrie's teeth on edge. "I just think . . ." Carrie stopped, searching for the right words. "I always brag about my parents, you know?" she finally said. "Because you guys actually haven't sold out the things you believe in—and that's how you raised me. But now it feels like it was all just a bunch of words. . . ."

"That's not true, Carrie," her dad said firmly. "And I'm sorry if we've disappointed you. Sometimes love takes precedence."

"I know, Dad," Carrie said softly. "I'm sorry. . . ." *I'm not being fair to them,* Carrie told herself. *I know they're trying to help.*

"We love you, sweetie," her father said, his voice full of emotion. "Okay," he finally added briskly. "We're off for home now. We should get to Teaneck by four this afternoon. Call us if you need us."

"Okay, Dad," Carrie said. "Bye." She hung up the kitchen phone at the Templetons' and leaned her head against the wall.

I'm getting to hate the telephone, she thought. *All it's been bringing me are problems. My parents leave telling me not to do anything foolish, and Ray calls last night telling me that his trip to Boston was a total*

waste of time. Thank you, New England Bell.
Thank you very much.

"Carrie! You ready to take me downtown?" Ian screamed running into the kitchen.

"Now?" she asked dully. The dirty dishes from breakfast still sat on the table, along with the remnants of Chloe's spilled glass of milk. Chloe was upstairs with her mother.

"Now!" Ian insisted. "Joe at the Smoke Shop said they get *Rock On* in at nine-thirty today—it's already nine-twenty!"

Carrie stared at Ian and had to smile. He was wearing his wraparound black sunglasses and a black nylon tour jacket over a pair of black jeans.

"You look very rock and roll," she told him.

"I do?" he asked eagerly, then immediately tried to cover his reaction. "I mean, this is my look, you know? Every star has a look."

"I see," Carrie said gravely, carrying the breakfast dishes over to the dishwasher.

"I thought this was good," Ian continued, "since Dad always gets real dressed up, you know, tuxes and stuff."

"Right," Carrie agreed distractedly, wiping up the spilled milk on the table.

"I wouldn't want people to confuse us or anything," Ian added.

"Good idea," Carrie nodded, and dumped the sponge in the sink. Ian looked so sincere, and so much younger than thirteen, that Carrie prayed this article in *Rock On* would say nice things about him. "Okay, let's hit the road," she told him, grabbing the car keys.

It was foggy out, and a light drizzle began as Carrie headed the car toward Joe's Smoke Shop. *What a great accompaniment to my mood,* Carrie thought glumly. *I should be excited about seeing my photos in* Rock On *but I can hardly even think about it right now.*

"This is gonna be so cool, so awesome," Ian chanted, practically rocking back and forth with excitement in the front seat next to Carrie. She parked the car, and Ian was out his door before she even reached for her door handle.

"Good morning, Joe!" Carrie said, as she made her way into his shop.

"Good morning yourself, Carrie," Joe said.

"Where's Ian?" Carrie asked, scanning the store. He was nowhere to be found.

Joe shrugged and pointed to a back storage room. "He grabbed *Rock On* and went back there."

"There's a story about him in it," Carrie said.

"So I understand," Joe said, with a strange look on his face. "The photo you took of him is really, well, interesting."

Odd, Carrie thought. *That's a peculiar expression on Joe's face.* She made her way to the back room. There was Ian, sitting on a straight back chair, his head buried in *Rock On* magazine.

He looked up at Carrie, and she saw his face was white as a sheet.

"Carrie," he said, his voice low and devoid of expression, "I am totally screwed."

Carrie hurried over to Ian and took the magazine from him. She sat down in the chair next to him and started to read. She looked at the headline and at the byline, and involuntarily let out a gasp.

LIKE FATHER, LIKE SON: THE TRAGEDY OF IAN TEMPLETON
by Faith O'Connor

Imagine, if you would for a moment, a rock and roll band with the inauspicious name of Lord Whitehead and the Zit People. At the same time, imagine that this band's musical intention—if you could call it that—is to demonstrate the moral and ethical bankruptcy of the post-industrial age. And they do it by smashing iron bars on the innards of old washing machines.

Imagine no more. This is how Ian Templeton, the wiry, thirteen-year-old son of cocaine-abusing rock icon Graham Perry has chosen to express his troubled and tormented soul. Years of being raised in his father's chemical-hazed shadow have left young Ian an egocentric and imperious child, far younger than his thirteen years.

They have also left him devoid of musical taste—not that he shares even a smidgen of his father's once-considerable musical ability.

Carrie stopped reading even though the article went on for several columns.

Oh my God, Carrie thought. *They've torn him to pieces! They handed him and Graham a bunch of garbage about what the article would be. And they manipulatively sent in Zetta Hunter to do the research, because they knew Graham would never let Faith*

137

O'Connor do the story—it's a classic hatchet job.

Then she looked to the top of the page, at the photos that accompanied the story.

Oh no. There's the picture I took of Ian looking totally supercilious. But what about the rest of these? Carrie thought. *I didn't take them.*

There were two other photographs on the same page. One was a picture of Ian backstage at one of his father's concerts, in a group with a bunch of kids. They all held hand-rolled cigarettes, including Ian. Carrie knew that what actually happened that night was that Claudia caught Ian smoking and grounded him for two weeks.

But to the world, Carrie realized, *it looks like Ian's smoking marijuana.*

The other picture was a shot of Ian and Graham together, the famous father towering over the son, Ian looking like a totally lost little boy.

Carrie looked up from the magazine and over at Ian.

"Oh, Ian . . ." she said softly.

He was crying.

"Hey, where's *Rock On?*" Carrie heard a kid asking in the front of the store. "Is the article about Ian in there?"

"Let me look!" another kid was saying excitedly.

Ian shot Carrie a miserable, panicked look.

Carrie looked around, thinking fast. "This way," she motioned. There was a back door that led out into an alley. Carrie and Ian hustled out and went the long way back to the car. *There's no reason he should have to face those kids until he's had time to digest all this,* Carrie thought, looking over at the boy's tear-stained face. *God, I loathe Faith O'Connor.* She and Ian walked quickly to the car and headed back for the Templetons'.

"My father's going to kill me," Ian sobbed, swiping at his cheeks with the back of his hand.

"No he's not," Carrie said. "You didn't write the article. Faith O'Connor did. It's not your fault."

"But he told me not to do it," Ian said, gulping hard.

"You can't blame yourself, Ian," Carrie said, turning the windshield wipers on higher to combat the hard-falling rain.

"I wish I could die right this minute," Ian said, staring out the window.

Carrie fought the urge to tell Ian that he didn't mean what he said. She knew how awful he felt, and she knew it would pass.

"What about the band?" Ian continued miserably. "They're gonna laugh at me!" His voice cracked. "They'll all quit!"

"They'll for sure know it wasn't your fault," Carrie said firmly. "They were right there!"

"And Becky," Ian continued as if he hadn't even heard Carrie. "What about Becky? I am totally screwed. None of them are gonna want to stay in the band, and Becky probably won't ever speak to me again."

"But Ian—"

"It's true!" Ian cried. "I'll be the joke of the island! I probably already am."

Carrie was silent. The worst part was that she knew that Ian was probably right about what Becky's reaction would be. *Becky has all the tact and sensitivity of the Terminator.*

That would be the most painful part of this ordeal for Ian.

When Carrie pulled into the Templeton's driveway, she could see through the beating windshield wipers, that someone was standing in front of the Templetons' front door, dressed in a yellow rain slicker.

"Omigod, it's Becky Jacobs," Ian said, slumping down in his seat. "Tell her I'm not here."

Carrie slowed the car to a stop. Becky ran toward them. Ian slid further down in his seat.

"Tell her I've thrown myself in the Atlantic," Ian whispered. He covered his head with his rain poncho.

"Ian?" Becky called, rapping her knuckles on his window. He sunk down lower in the seat.

"She knows you're under the poncho," Carrie said softly.

"Ian, my friend Mindy called me from Providence and read me the article!"

No reply.

"Ian!" Becky repeated irritably. She opened

his car door and stuck her head into the car.

Ian lifted his face. It was flushed with embarrassment. He turned to Becky, looking like a lamb ready for slaughter.

"I'll leave you guys alone to talk," Carrie said, reaching for the door handle.

"No, you can hear this," Becky said. "Your pictures were part of the article."

"I know," Carrie said with a sigh.

"Faith O'Connor is such a bitch," Becky said, her eyes shining.

"Wha . . . what?" Ian stammered.

"She's a bitch!" Becky repeated vehemently. "She's an old washed-up over-the-hill two-bit know-nothing who thinks she's cool beans but she's really cold crap!"

"She is?" Ian asked faintly.

"I know why she wrote those awful things about you," Becky said, the rain flattening her long brown hair. "Because she knows that we're important, but she's afraid to admit it!"

"She is?" Ian asked again, barely peeking out of the top of his poncho.

"Of course!" Becky exclaimed. "Because she

is part of the problem, not part of the solution!"

Carrie saw Ian start to smile. "Yeah," he said, "that's right."

"And when we get our big record deal," Becky continued triumphantly, "I'm gonna take this article, wrap it around some road-kill, and send it to her!"

Will wonders never cease, Carrie thought to herself, looking over at Becky with admiration.

"Cool idea," Ian managed to say casually, getting out of the car.

Carrie got out from her side and hurried through the rain toward the house. Just as she was opening the front door, she glanced at Ian and Becky, standing near the car in the rain.

Becky leaned over and kissed Ian smack on the lips, and then she ran to her friend's car which was waiting in the street.

Carrie and Ian walked in the door together, Ian in a daze.

"I said no comment and I mean no comment," Graham was barking into the phone.

"We'll have a prepared statement later." He hung up. The phone rang again. This time he let it ring.

"Hi Dad," Ian said sheepishly, walking into the living room. Carrie followed him and saw Claudia sitting on the couch.

"Ian," Graham said, smiling just a little bit, "welcome to the world of bigtime rock and roll."

"How are you doing?" Claudia asked her son softly.

"Pretty awful," Ian admitted. "But at least Becky doesn't hate me. How'd you find out about the article?"

"The phone started ringing two minutes after you left," Graham said, "and it hasn't stopped since."

As if to validate his words, the phone rang again.

"It's driving me nuts," Claudia said, putting her hands over her ears.

Suddenly, the fax machine in the next room sounded off.

"We're expecting a transmission from my publicist in New York," Graham told them.

"I'll get it," Carrie offered, and hurried into the office for the fax. She read it as she brought it back into the room. It was a draft of a prepared statement from Graham Perry to the media.

"Read it out loud," Graham asked Carrie when she walked back into the living room. "I want to hear it."

Carrie read the statement in a clear voice.

FROM: Mr. Graham Perry, Freedom Recording Artist

TO: Members of the Media

RE: *Rock On* magazine article about my son, Ian Templeton

My wife, Claudia, and I are disgusted and appalled by the article about our son Ian that appears in the current issue of *Rock On* magazine. Not only did *Rock On* violate journalistic ethics in its effort to secure the story, but the story itself and the photographs that accompany it are libelous. On the advice of counsel, Claudia and I will be filing suit in Federal

District Court, Southern District of New York, this afternoon. The defendants in the lawsuit will be *Rock On* magazine in its corporate capacity, and the author of the article, Faith O'Connor. Claudia and I believe this utterly false story deserves no further comment and therefore we will issue no other statements.

"Wow," said Ian. "You're going to give that to the press?"

"Absolutely," Graham said. "That story cut you to shreds. No way are we letting that rag get away with this."

"How long until the case gets to court?" Ian asked.

"Ian, the point is not whether we win the suit," Graham said, sounding a little annoyed.

"Graham," Claudia said, "how is he supposed to know that?"

"You're right," Graham said, rubbing the day's growth of stubble on his chin. "Ian, sit down. I want to explain something to you. You too, Carrie. One of your photos is in this thing—and take the damned phone off the hook."

Carrie removed the receiver and then sat down next to Ian on the couch.

"I hope you learn something from this," Graham said to his son.

"I did," Ian said earnestly. "I mean, I should never have said I wanted them to do the story—"

Graham cut him off with a wave of his hand. "Wrong, Ian. They would have done this story with you or without you," he said. "It was easier with you, that's all."

"But how?" Ian asked. "I don't get it."

"They would have sent a reporter here, interviewed your friends, gone through our damned garbage if they felt like it," Graham said bitterly. "They would have talked to kids who go to school with you—found some kid who doesn't like you. And that would have been that."

"But Dad—"

"Sometimes Ian," Graham said steadily, "there are things that happen in this life that are bigger than you. Bigger than me. Things you can't control."

"This isn't the first time we've been through something like this," his mother pointed out.

"Do you know what I feel worst about, son?" Graham asked Ian.

Ian shook his head. "No, what?"

"This is my fault," Graham said softly. "If it weren't for me, they would never have done this hatchet job on you."

And then Carrie saw an amazing thing. Graham Perry, rock icon, the man for whom Billy Joel opened shows, the man who the world considered a music legend, started to cry.

TEN

Two hours later, Carrie lay on her bed staring at the ceiling. She had turned off the ringer on her telephone so that the influx of calls from the media was somewhat less annoying. And she tried to think. Hard.

For a couple of hours, she had actually managed to not think about Ray. But now as she lay on her bed, all the anxiety came rushing back.

I have until midafternoon to decide whether to marry Ray, she thought. *That's when I'm meeting him at the Play Café, and I can't put it off any longer. I can't believe I have absolutely no idea what I'm going to do.*

Carrie heard the phone ring downstairs yet again. She heard Graham read his prepared statement for about the fortieth time that day.

"Carrie?" Claudia Templeton called from downstairs.

Carrie sat up. "Yes, Claudia?" she answered.

"We're going to call-forward our phone to Graham's publicist in New York. We're getting sick and tired of saying the same thing over and over again." Claudia said from the bottom of the stairs. "So if you're expecting anyone to call you, you ought to call them now."

Only Emma, Carrie thought. *She said she'd call me at one-thirty. I'd better get her on the phone now.*

"I'm gonna make a quick call," she yelled down to Claudia, and then she padded back to the phone and dialed Emma's number.

Emma answered on the third ring. "Hello, Hewitt residence, Emma Cresswell speaking."

"Hi, it's me," Carrie said, stretching out on her bed.

"How are you holding up?" Emma asked. "I

can only talk a little while—Wills and his friend Stinky are doing science experiments in the basement, and Jane asked me to make sure they don't blow the place up."

"I'm okay, I guess," Carrie answered. "Did you hear about the disaster with *Rock On*."

"Yeah, Sam called me about an hour ago— you know word travels fast on this island. Poor Ian!"

"He seems to be taking it pretty well," Carrie said. "Graham's the one who's upset."

"How about you?" Emma asked Carrie.

"About *Rock On?*" Carrie responded.

"About Ray," Emma said.

Carrie was silent for a moment. She glanced outside; rain was pelting the window. "I'm totally confused," Carrie admitted. "In two hours, I'm going to be sitting across from Ray in the Play Café, and I'm going to tell him whether I'm going to marry him."

"Have you made up your mind?" Emma queried.

"Nope," Carrie said. "I feel like I'm all tied up in knots! I need some words of wisdom."

"Me? Words of wisdom for you?" Emma

asked. "Now, that's ironic. You're the one who always has words of wisdom for me!"

"Well, I'm not feeling so wise right now," Carrie said. "I keep picturing it in my mind. There I am, sitting across from Ray in the stupid Play Café, and I tell him I can't marry him. How can I do that, when I know it could literally kill him?"

"It's so strange," Emma mused. "I mean, even though I know the political situation in his country, it doesn't seem real, does it?"

"That's part of the problem," Carrie remarked. "Everytime I say that this is a life or death situation, it just sounds so melodramatic!"

"But it's not," Emma said.

"No, it's not," Carrie agreed. "It's just that we can't imagine that stuff here in America."

"I don't know," Emma said, making a stab at humor. "My parents tend to think of the Democrats as terrorists."

"Funny, that's how my parents look at Republicans," Carrie replied.

There was silence on the phone.

This is one time humor isn't going to make

it any easier, Carrie realized sadly. "I just wish someone could tell me the right thing to do," Carrie said softly.

This time Emma was silent for a moment. "I wish I could do that," Emma finally said. "But I can't. No one knows the right thing for you to do but you. You know what I think."

Yep, I know what she thinks, Carrie considered. *She thinks that I should do everything I can for Ray, short of marrying him.*

"I know," Carrie said. "But—"

"I'll tell you this," Emma interrupted. "No matter what you decide to do, I'll always be your best friend. You can count on that. You can count on me."

Carrie felt tears well up in her eyes as she listened to her friend. She sniffed them back.

"Thanks Emma. That's important to me. I'll call you later."

"Okay, Carrie," Emma said. "You can call me anytime you want. Bye."

Carrie hung up the phone.

Damn. I'm no closer to figuring out what to do than I was before I called her. And it's almost time to decide.

* * *

"Hi, Carrie!" Patsi called out as she picked up two orders of burgers from the kitchen.

"Hi," Carrie replied, closing her umbrella.

"I love this weather—the place is practically deserted," Patsi said as she sailed by with the plates of food. She served them to the only party in the place, other than Ray, who sat by himself in the back.

Carrie's heart pounded in her chest as she made her way back to the booth.

"Hi," she said, sliding in across from him.

"You look kind of like a drowned puppy," he told her with a fond smile.

"It's pouring," Carrie replied. She stared at her friend.

"So," she finally said.

"So," he said.

They both knew why they were there.

"Any news from your father?" Carrie asked hopefully.

"None," Ray said grimly. "I heard on CNN that the new government has applied for recognition from the United Nations."

"Is that good or bad?" Carrie asked.

"Bad," Ray replied tersely. "If they are recognized by other nations, it will be impossible to get rid of them."

"Do you think the United Nations will recognize them?" Carrie asked.

"I don't have the luxury of thinking," Ray said. "I just pray."

In that moment, Carrie made up her mind.

"Ray?" she said. "I'll do it." She looked him right in the eye. "I'll marry you."

He stared at her for a moment. "No."

"Yes," Carrie replied. "I've given it a lot of thought. It's the right thing to do."

"For whom?" Ray asked pointedly.

"For . . . for you," Carrie replied.

"But not you," Ray said.

"If you mean am I in love with you, the answer is no," Carrie said. "But you already know that. If you're asking me if I'm scared, the answer is yes—but you already know that, too."

"I don't want you to regret it for the rest of your life," Ray said.

Carrie shook her head. "I won't," she said.

"How do you know that?" Ray asked.

"Okay, I don't know that!" Carrie exclaimed. "But I just can't think that far ahead now!"

"And what about Billy?" Ray pressed. "You love him!"

"Ray, why are you making this more difficult?" Carrie demanded. "Stop it!"

"I can't!" Ray cried out with passion. "You shouldn't have to make such a choice for your life!"

"Right," Carrie agreed. Suddenly she felt very tired and very old. "But here it is, anyway."

Ray sat silently. "You are going to have to change your entire life for me," he finally said, pain etched in his dark eyes. "Nothing will be the same."

The couple across the room burst out laughing, and the girl got up to put some coins in the juke box. *Was I really that carefree just a few days ago?* Carrie thought. But now everything was different. She wondered if she'd ever be like that again.

"Look, Ray," Carrie said, turning back to her friend. "This isn't a . . . a totally black or white thing. There're a million reasons I shouldn't do this, but there's a bigger reason why I should. And I've made up my mind. So let's figure out exactly what we're going to do."

"Your parents will kill you," Ray said softly. "But I am now the most grateful person on earth." Tears welled up in his eyes.

Carrie reached across the table for his hand, and a wave of emotion overcame her. Tears began to stream down her face.

For a brief moment, both she and Ray sat there crying. Patsi walked by and gave them a curious look. Carrie paid her no mind. Finally, she and Ray both took paper napkins with the Play Café logo on them and dried their tears.

Ray pocketed his napkin. "Souvenir," he told her, attempting a smile.

"So what do we have to do?" Carrie asked.

"We need to talk to Jane and Jeff Hewitt," Ray suggested. "They are my lawyers."

Oh my God, Carrie thought. *Lawyers. It's real now. It's really going to happen. I'm so scared! I don't want to do this! I don't want to lose Billy!* Then she resolutely banished such thoughts from her mind. *I've decided and I'm going to do whatever I need to.*

"I think you will need to leave your job here," Ray continued. "We must establish a residence together."

Carrie nodded dully. *Leave my job. Okay. No problem. The Templetons will hate me forever.*

"I think New Haven would be best," Ray suggested.

"So we can stay in college," Carrie said flatly.

"Yes," Ray said.

Carrie thought for a moment about how complicated her life was about to become. Then she spoke. "There's one thing we need to do first," she said.

"Anything," Ray answered.

"We need to go talk to Billy," Carrie replied. "Together. Right now."

On the way over to Billy's house, Carrie had second thoughts about whether she should break the news with Ray at her side.

Finally, she decided to drop him off at the Sunset Inn, and have him take the trolley to Billy's after a half-hour or so.

That'll give me a while to talk to Billy alone, Carrie thought. *Not that it's going to make things any easier.*

Carrie dropped Ray off and drove to the house that Billy shared with the other members of Flirting With Danger. She parked in front and stared at the weathered house, remembering all the terrific times she'd had there.

Oh Billy, she prayed. *Please. You have to understand. I'll die if I lose you. . . .*

She forced herself to get out of the car, glad it had finally stopped raining. The door swung open before she could knock. Billy was waiting for her.

Billy hugged her tightly, then held her at arms' length, his eyes searching hers. "You've decided," he finally said. *That's not a question,* Carrie thought, *that's a statement. He knows.*

"Yes."

"You're going to marry him," Billy said flatly.

"Yes."

A terrible look of pain flitted across Billy's face. In that moment, Carrie wanted to take back her decision more than she'd ever wanted anything in her life.

Without a word, Billy led Carrie by the hand into the familiar living room. It was full of slightly run-down furniture. Rock and roll posters covered the walls. Carrie thought she'd never seen such a lovely room in her life.

"So you're going to do it," Billy said softly, sitting next to her on the worn couch.

"Yes," Carrie replied. "I have to."

"That's not true," Billy said pointedly. "You want to."

"Do I?" Carrie asked. "I don't feel like I want to."

"Then don't!" Billy said sharply.

"I didn't come here to discuss it," Carrie said. "I've already made up my mind."

"Well, then I guess there's nothing to say." Billy turned his head away from Carrie.

"There is," Carrie insisted, putting her hand on his cheek. He turned back to her. "I love you, Billy. I still want us to be together."

"Oh yeah," Billy said bitterly. "Well, I don't mess around with married women."

"But it's not like that!" Carrie protested, feeling as if a knife were cutting into her heart.

"No, I guess it's not," Billy admitted. "But God, Carrie, I feel like I'm losing you. . . ."

"You're not," she assured him. "We can make it work! I know we can!"

A small smile came to Billy's lips. "The damned thing is, Carrie Alden, that what I love about you is exactly what made you decide to do this for Ray."

For the third time that day Carrie felt tears well up in her eyes. She couldn't stop them. Soon she was crying uncontrollably. Then she was in Billy's arms, kissing him and crying like she hadn't cried since she was ten years old and had found her pet cat dead in the family basement.

"It's going to be okay for us," Carrie assured him between shuddering sobs. "It has to be!"

"We'll try," Billy said, holding her close.

"I'll make sure of it!" Carrie vowed.

"How?" Billy asked, pulling back to look at her tear-streaked face. "What if you go away for a weekend with me the day the INS decides to pay you a visit? What if someone sees us together? What if—"

"We'll be careful!" Carrie cried. "They won't be watching Ray and me every minute! We're not criminals!"

"I'm just not going to paint some kind of rosy picture of this," Billy said, "because it sucks. I don't know what's going to happen, and neither do you." He reached behind him on the table and plucked up a few Kleenex for Carrie. She blew her nose noisily.

"I admire what you're doing, Car," Billy said softly, rubbing his knuckles gently across her cheek. "And I know why you decided to do this. I just wish that it didn't have to be you."

The doorbell rang. Billy got up to get it.

"It's Ray," Carrie said. "I told him to come over."

Billy sighed, shrugged, and went to get the door.

The two guys regarded each other for a moment. They were complete physical opposites—Billy, with his tall, rangy physique, and Ray, shorter and more muscular, with his snappingly handsome dark eyes and curly hair.

"You have the most wonderful girlfriend in the world," Ray finally said.

Billy stared at him silently.

"Someday, when I can go back home to Matalan," Ray continued earnestly, "I hope to meet a woman like Carrie."

"Why should you have to, when you'll already be married to the real thing?" Billy asked bluntly.

"Because Carrie is in love with you," Ray said simply. "That is how it is, and how it will remain."

Billy made an approving sound. "Come on in."

Ray followed Billy into the living room. Billy indicated a chair, and Ray sat down. Billy sat next to Carrie.

"I'm not going to beat around the bush, Ray," Billy said, nervously drumming his fingers on the coffee table. He stopped himself and folded his arms. "I'm not happy about this at all."

"I understand," Ray replied.

"Yeah," Billy said. He looked at Carrie, then back at Ray. "I understand why Carrie feels she has to marry you, but I hate it, just the same."

"As I would, were I in your shoes," Ray said with dignity. "It is not easy to be the boyfriend of a married girl. But I assure you—"

"You assure me what?" Billy asked hotly. "That she'll still be my girlfriend? That I'll see her whenever I want? That nothing is going to change between us? That you'll never try to put any moves on her?" He snorted in disgust, then shook his head.

"I can assure you of your final point," Ray said solemnly. "You have my word on this."

"What am I, a loaf of bread?" Carrie interrupted. "You two act as if I don't have a mind of my own."

"I did not mean to imply—" Ray began.

"My relationship with Ray is strictly platonic and that won't change," Carrie said firmly.

"Living in one apartment, maybe even in one bedroom?" Billy questioned darkly.

"Yes!" Carrie shot back.

"I never knew a guy and a girl who could really stay platonic friends," Billy said. "Unless they just weren't attracted to each other."

"Well, now you do," Carrie said.

Billy stared at her. "Does that mean that you're attracted to him?"

"Stop it!" Carrie cried, jumping up. "This is stupid!"

"I'm sorry," Billy said with a sigh. "Sit down. Please. This is not easy for me."

"It's not easy for any of us, Billy," Carrie said, sitting back down next to him. She ran her fingers through her hair. "God, I'm losing it."

Ray looked first at Carrie and then at Billy. "I want you both to know I am deeply, deeply sorry to be the cause of any troubles between the two of you." He looked at Carrie. "And

Carrie, you are one of the most courageous women I have ever met in my life."

"I don't feel very courageous," Carrie replied in a tremulous voice.

"There are not many people who would do what you are about to do," Ray said quietly.

"I know," Billy agreed sadly. He gave her a look that broke her heart. "She's just trying to do what's right."

Carrie leaned over and kissed Billy, and he put his arm around her and pulled her close. Carrie closed her eyes and reveled in the feeling of security in Billy's arms, even though it was only for the moment.

And she couldn't help worrying, even as she lingered in Billy's embrace, if she was about to make the single worst mistake of her entire life.

ELEVEN

"We're going to miss you, Carrie," Claudia said sadly.

"Very much," Graham added. "You've been great with the kids."

Carrie nodded, feeling sad. Four days earlier she'd gathered up all her courage and told the Templetons she was leaving to marry Ray Saliverez—even as she'd said it, it seemed totally unreal to her—as if she were speaking about someone else. At first Graham and Claudia had been shocked, but when she explained why she was doing what she was doing, they'd finally understood. Now, here she was, on her last day as their au pair.

Tomorrow I'm actually marrying Ray and moving back to New Haven, Carrie told herself. Still, no matter how many times this same sentence went through her head, it didn't seem any more real than the time before.

"You've been so nice about this," Carrie told them earnestly, fiddling with the place mat on the kitchen table. Ever since she'd made the decision to marry Ray she'd been so nervous—it seemed as if her hands and her feet were always moving with nervous energy. Now she willed herself to sit still.

"Hey, as sorry as we are to lose you, we understand," Graham said, sipping his coffee. "I can't tell you how many people I know who were in green-card marriages during the seventies and eighties. It's not that odd a thing."

"It is to me," Carrie said quietly.

"I imagine so," Claudia said warmly, leaning forward in her chair. "I don't know many kids with the guts to do what you're doing."

"I don't know if it's guts . . ." Carrie said. *Or stupidity,* she finished in her own mind.

"Carrie, Billy's here," Ian said from the doorway.

Carrie sprang up out of her chair. "Do you mind—?"

"Go," Claudia said with a smile.

She found Billy sitting on a weathered cedar bench on the far side of the front lawn.

"Hi," she said softly, sitting down next to him.

"I wasn't going to come. . . ." Billy said, staring out into the distance, his hands dangling between his knees.

"I'm so glad you did," Carrie said fervently.

"Tomorrow's the big day, huh."

"Yeah," Carrie agreed. "Everything is so strange—nothing seems real."

"I keep telling myself I understand," Billy said, not looking at Carrie, "and I do. But this other part of me feels like punching Raymond Saliverez in the face—what a jerk I am, huh?"

Carrie didn't say anything. She just leaned her head against his shoulder. They were silent for a long time.

"I thought I had something to say when I came here," Billy finally mumbled. "But I don't. You're not about to change your mind."

"I gave my word," Carrie said.

"Un-give it," Billy said fiercely.

"I can't," Carrie whispered. "You know I can't."

"Yeah," Billy said, his voice gruff with emotion.

"It won't be forever, Billy," Carrie promised him fervently.

"How long?" Billy demanded. "More than a month? More than a year?"

"I don't know," Carrie admitted. "Long enough to make sure Ray's safe."

"Real noble," Billy replied sarcastically. He ran his hand over his face. "I'm sorry. That was a crappy thing to say. I better leave before I mess this up completely."

Billy started to get up.

"No, don't go," Carrie pleaded. She gently pulled him back down onto the bench. "Billy, I love you. Nothing is going to change."

She put her arms around him and kissed him until she could feel him passionately returning her kiss. He kissed her hard—as if he wanted to imprint her mouth with his lips forever—then he pulled away.

"I love you too, Carrie," he said in a ragged

voice. "But I don't believe in fairy tales. Everything is going to change."

Then he got up from the bench, and without a backwards glance, he walked away.

In between crying spells, Carrie tried to get ready to meet Sam and Emma on the beach. They had called that morning and asked—no, ordered—her to meet them. She was in such a weird state of mind that she felt as if she were moving through molasses.

Maybe it's all just some terrible dream, she thought, as she splashed cold water on her tear-stained face. *I never said I'd marry Ray, and Billy didn't walk away from me an hour ago as if we were through.* The memory of that sent fresh agony coursing through Carrie's heart and she started crying all over again.

"Can I come in?" Ian asked shyly from the doorway.

"Sure," Carrie said, wiping her eyes and trying to look as if she was in control.

Ian came in and leaned against her desk. "I wanted to tell you . . ." he began.

"Yes?" Carrie said, sitting down on her bed.

"That, um . . . Chloe is really going to miss you," Ian said, staring hard at the pattern in the area rug.

Carrie bit her lip. "I'll miss her, too. But I'll miss you even more."

Ian looked at her sharply. "You will?"

Carrie nodded. "I think you're pretty terrific."

"Oh," Ian said, going back to looking at the carpet. He fumbled with something in the back pocket of his jeans. "This is kinda this stupid song I wrote," he mumbled. "I mean, in case the Zits ever decide to do originals, which we won't." He thrust the piece of paper at her.

She unfolded it and saw song lyrics, and the song's title, "Carrie's Smile."

"Well, I gotta motor," Ian said, and fled from her room as fast as he could get out the door.

"Unbelievable," Carrie said under her breath. Then she read Ian's song.

CARRIE'S SMILE

Some days I feel real good

But it only lasts for a while
Some days I feel real sad
But it's better when I see Carrie smile.

Even though she's leaving
Gonna go walk down that aisle
When I get to feeling bad
I remember Carrie's smile.

Carrie's smile
Carrie's smile
I remember Carrie's smile.

"Oh God, Ian . . ." Carrie said out loud. And she couldn't help the tears from falling again. She folded up the paper and put it in her jewelry box—it was something that she knew she'd cherish forever. Then she resolutely washed her face one more time, ran a brush through her hair, and ran down the stairs to go meet her friends on the beach.

"I gotta hand it to you, Carrie," Sam said when Carrie plopped down in the sand next to her a short while later. "This is as bad as I've ever seen you look."

"Thank you so much," Carrie said. Her eyes were so swollen from crying that she felt as if she was looking at the world through tiny slits.

"You do look awful," Emma agreed, a look of concern washing over her face.

"Well, I feel awful," Carrie said.

"Maybe you shouldn't do this then . . ." Emma began.

"Stop!" Carrie said, putting her hands over her ears. "It's happening, and that's all there is to it!"

Emma nodded. "Okay." She picked up a handful of sand and let it fall through her fingers. "So, what did your parents have to say?"

"Yeah, did they promise to kill you when you went back to New Haven, or are they coming up here to do the deed?" Sam joked lamely.

"They weren't too pleased about it, that's for sure," Carrie said.

"So what did they say?" Emma persisted.

"The party line, which is—" Carrie paused for dramatic effect, "you are old enough to make your own decisions . . . even if those decisions stink!"

"They did not actually say that!" Sam cried.

Carrie grinned sadly. "All except the last part," she admitted.

"Where's Ray?" Emma asked.

"More importantly, where's Billy?" Sam added.

"Ray's in Portland taking care of some paperwork with Jane and Jeff—they've been great, Emma, I've got to tell you—they're not even charging Ray anything for their work—and Billy's gone to the Sound Store in Falmouth," Carrie said bitterly, "to take care of an amp."

"He'll come around," Sam assured Carrie, scratching a mosquito bite on her arm. "He's crazed for you."

Carrie looked at her friend and smiled. Today Sam was wearing cut-offs and a Minnie Mouse Disney World T-shirt, with her red hair sticking out the back of a red-and-white polka-dot baseball cap.

"You look like Woody Woodpecker in that hat," Emma pointed out.

"I do not," Sam said cooly. "I look incredibly cute."

"Sure," Emma teased her. "Pretty much irresistible."

Carrie looked at her two friends. They were trying so hard to be cheerful, to help keep her spirits up. "I really love you guys," she said softly.

"Well, of course," Sam replied. "We're the most lovable—which is how I know you're going to love our big idea."

"What big idea?" Carrie asked.

Sam looked at Emma, who shrugged nonchalantly. "You tell her," she told Sam.

"Okay," Sam said. "You're getting an engagement party."

"A *what?!*" Carrie exclaimed.

"Engagement party," Emma said simply. "For the shortest engagement in the history of Sunset Island."

"For what we hope is the shortest marriage in the history of the United States!" Sam added fervently.

"But . . . look, it's really nice of you, honest," Carrie said, sounding as flustered as she felt. "But I don't want an engagement party."

"Yes, you do," Sam said easily. "You only think you don't."

"No, I really don't," Carrie said. "I'd feel like an idiot! It's not like this is a real marriage—"

"So, we'll make it a fake party," Sam said airily.

"No you guys, really—" Carrie protested.

"It's tonight," Emma said, "at the Play Café, starting at nine o'clock."

"Wear something scandalous," Sam suggested.

"It just doesn't feel right," Carrie insisted, "having an engagement party—"

"Because this isn't what you had in mind when you thought about getting engaged, right?" Emma finished Carrie's sentence for her.

Carrie nodded sadly.

"Listen, girlfriend. We got that part," Sam said, pulling her knees up to her chin. "But the way we look at it is—we can spend the last night before you get married either laughing or crying."

"And we've decided you've cried enough," Emma finished softly.

Carrie managed a small smile. "Looks like I don't have much choice."

"Looks like you're right!" Sam said. "Yowza! Check that guy out." A tanned guy with long blond hair jogged by. "Fox-o-licious!"

Carrie laughed in spite of herself. "Honestly, Sam, you never change!"

"That's the whole idea, babe," Sam said, putting her arm around Carrie. "No matter what happens, some things—like the three of us, for example—are forever."

"I second that," Emma said softly.

"You two are the greatest friends in the world," Carrie said.

"Glad you think so," Sam said, her eyes still following the guy on the beach. "Excuse me, I've got to go invite that guy to the party!"

"Sam!" Carrie laughed. "You are incorrigible!"

"Too true," Sam agreed. "Like I said, some things are forever!"

TWELVE

It had taken some big-time convincing on Carrie's part to engineer it, but Carrie, Ray, and Billy all walked into the Play Café together. First Sam had called both guys, then Emma had stopped over at Billy's, and then Carrie had called Billy. Knowing that Billy had finally agreed gave Carrie a little ray of hope—she would find some way to keep their relationship going, no matter what it took.

When the three of them arrived, the party was already in full swing. It seemed like the whole island was there—word about Carrie and Ray had traveled fast. Hot dance music was playing through the Play Café sound system, and a huge group of people were already boogying on the café dance floor.

"Yo! Carrie!" Carrie heard Sam call to her just a few seconds after she walked in.

"Hi," Carrie said, hugging Sam as if she hadn't seen her for days.

"You okay?" Sam said in her ear.

Carrie nodded.

"So, how are the two luckiest guys on the island?" Sam asked Billy and Ray.

Billy gave her a stormy look; Ray attempted a smile.

"Whoa, we need some serious mood alterations here!" Sam yelled over the music.

"Hey pardner, you doin' all right?" Pres said, ambling over to drape one arm across Billy's shoulders.

"I've been better, man," Billy admitted.

"Let's go," Pres said. "I'll bring him back," he said to Carrie over his shoulder. She scanned the crowd. "Where's Emma?"

"Over by the stage," Sam said. "You cool here for a sec, Ray? I need Carrie."

"I'm fine," Ray assured her.

Sam and Carrie threaded their way through the crowd to where Emma was standing.

"You look like you're waiting for a servant to fetch you tea," Sam teased Emma when they got there.

"I am," Emma teased back. She smiled at Carrie. "You hanging in there?"

Carrie nodded. "Pretty much. But it feels really strange to be here."

"Well, we're glad to see you!" Emma said gently.

"Where's Kurt?" Carrie asked, scanning the crowd.

"Driving," Emma said. "He said he'd come by around eleven."

Just then some girl in her early twenties with short black hair, wearing a daisy-print minidress walked up to Carrie.

"Carrie?"

"Yes?"

"Listen. I just wanted to tell you how much I admire you," she said fervently.

"Me?" Carrie asked.

"Absolutely," the girl said, fiddling with an earring. "I mean, you are like, so courageous."

"Oh," Carrie said lamely. "Well thanks."

"See ya," the girl said, and melted back into the crowd.

"Who was that?" Carrie asked.

"I think she's—" Emma began.

"Carrie?"

Carrie turned around and saw a tall couple, both very blond, staring at her expectantly.

"Yes?"

"We just had to say that you are the coolest," the girl gushed.

"The coolest," her boyfriend echoed. "We really admire you." They turned around and walked away, locked in each other's arms.

Everyone knows about me and Ray, Carrie thought. *Everyone's coming up to me to tell me that they think I'm some kind of a hero for marrying Ray. I think they're doing it because they are afraid that they wouldn't be willing to do the same thing. Am I a hero, or am I an idiot?*

"I think this crowd is about to name you Pope," Sam teased her.

"Isn't it bizarre?" Carrie said. "How did they all find out I'm marrying Ray to protect him anyway? I don't even know these people!"

She stood on her tiptoes to see over the crowd, looking for Billy. She saw him hanging out with Pres under one of the video monitors. And then she saw Ray under siege from the first girl who had approached her and told her she was a hero.

Looks like Billy and Ray didn't exactly decide to hang out the whole night together, she thought to herself.

"There's Darcy!" Emma said, pulling Carrie out of her thoughts. "I was hoping she and Molly would come."

"I'll get her attention," Sam said, waving frantically above the crowd. "Yo! Laken!" she yelled. Then she whistled between her teeth the way Darcy had taught her.

"Cool whistle," Darcy said with a laugh when she made her way over to them.

"Is Molly here?" Emma asked.

"I sure am," Molly said, wheeling herself through the crowd.

"I'm so glad you came," Carrie told her sincerely. She knew that Molly hated going to parties—any place that she thought people would stare at her.

"Hey, I figure at this party you're more of an oddity than I am," Molly teased. "I really admire what you're doing, by the way."

"You too?" Carrie said with a groan.

"What?" Molly looked blank.

"Everyone's been telling her that," Emma explained.

"So forget the brave heroine stuff," Sam ordered. "Molly, you look hot!"

"Thanks," Molly said happily. She had obviously made an effort for the party—she had put on black jeans, black cowboy boots, a white short-sleeve silk shirt with red embroidery on the shoulders, and a black bolero hat with embroidery similar to the shirt's.

"Wow, this place is hopping!" Darcy said, bopping to the old Doors tape that was blasting through the sound system.

"I'm getting out of the line of fire," Molly said, as a dancing couple practically tripped over her wheelchair. She started to wheel herself toward the wall, then turned around to Carrie. "No kidding, Carrie, I really do think you're courageous."

Carrie watched as Molly wheeled herself in the direction of the bar.

"I'll go with her," Darcy said. "Catch ya later!"

Yeah, right. Molly admiring my courage . . . Carrie thought, watching Molly's slow progress across the room. *She's the one with the courage! She's the one who—*

"Well, well, well, if it isn't the star of *Love Connection* herself!" chirped a familiar voice.

Carrie's stomach did a flip-flop as she turned to look at the girl who delivered this barbed comment. Of course it was Diana De Witt. Diana was wearing a white suede mini-skirt with a short, low-cut, sleeveless white suede shirt, and even Carrie had to admit that she looked devastating.

"Diana, what a surprise," Emma said. "I don't recall inviting you to this party."

"It must have been an oversight," Diana said. "Very careless of you."

"Silly me," Emma murmured, her voice dripping with sarcasm.

"I had to come anyway," Diana said, "to tell Carrie here how much I admire her courage."

Carrie stared hard at Diana. The expression on Diana's face remained simple and sincere.

What's this? Carrie asked herself. *Is it possible that Diana De Witt actually has a conscience? I mean, I'm sick of people saying how courageous I am, but coming from her, it's a small miracle.*

"Well thank you, Diana," Carrie said. "It's kind of you to—"

"Did I understand correctly that you and Ray are going to be living in Connecticut?" Diana asked innocently.

"That's right," Carrie said. "We both go to Yale."

"I see," Diana said, nodding. "And you're leaving right away?"

"Yes," Carrie said. "We've got to find an apartment and—"

"Well," Diana said, her voice filled with chirpy enthusiasm. "I guess that means you're not going to be around for the rest of the summer."

"Oh, I'm planning to visit already—" Carrie started to explain.

Diana smiled brightly. "Isn't it nice to know that Billy is going to be in good hands while you're gone?"

A dark feeling clutched at Carrie's throat. "What do you mean?"

"Well, he's in the band, I'm in the band, and you are in New Haven," Diana explained, as if she were talking to an idiot. "What a pity!"

I'm going to kill her, Carrie thought to herself. *She deserves to die.*

Carrie saw Sam come back from the bar just before Diana made this last remark. Sam stood right behind Diana with her drink in her hand.

"Oh Diana?" Sam said, tapping her on the shoulder.

"Oh Sammie! My favorite bandmate!" Diana chirped, turning to give Sam a malicious grin.

"I brought you a drink," Sam said.

And then she threw the drink, a green-colored concoction, right in Diana De Witt's face.

It dribbled from Diana's face down into her

considerable cleavage, on to the expensive white suede shirt, and down onto the floor.

"You bitch!" Diana shrieked, staring down at herself in shock.

"Oops!" Sam said innocently. "How clumsy of me! I was only aiming at your face, but I got it all over you!"

Diana screamed and lunged at Sam, who stepped easily out of her way. The people near Diana were snickering behind their hands—a lot of them were happy to see Diana De Witt get busted.

"You're dead!" Diana screamed at Sam. "Do you hear me? Dead!"

"I am everything! I am the coolest! And De Witt is the greenest!" Sam yelled triumphantly, jumping up and down with glee.

That cracked everyone up, and Sam was still singing when she danced across the room to throw her arms around Pres.

Diana grabbed a napkin off a table and wiped herself in futility. Then she marched across the room and grabbed Sam, swinging her around. She pulled her arm back to hit Sam—who was actually taken by surprise—

but Pres stepped in and twisted Diana's arm behind her back.

"Not nice," Pres chided Diana.

"Let me go, you stupid redneck!" Diana screamed, struggling against Pres's hold.

"Hey, hey, hey," Willie, the bouncer said, hurrying over to the scene. "What's going on?"

"That bitch threw a drink at me!" Diana screeched. "Look at my outfit! It's ruined!"

Willie could see that what Diana said was true: Her hair and shirt were wet and dripping green liquid, and Sam just stood there looking smug and not denying anything.

"Sorry babe. You're outta here," he told Sam.

"Me?" Sam asked incredulously. "But—"

Willie didn't listen as he hustled Sam out the front door.

"I don't care! It was worth it!" Sam was screaming, as the heavy door shut behind her.

Diana smiled bitchily and headed for the ladies room to clean up.

Carrie looked at Emma, who was standing

next to her. "Do you believe what just happened?"

"No!" Emma said vehemently. "Come with me." Emma marched over to Willie, Carrie in tow, and tapped him on his bulging bicep. "Excuse me," she said.

"Yeah?" Willie asked, staring down at the diminutive Emma.

"You just threw my friend out."

"And?" Willie asked.

"She is one of the hosts of this party," Emma said pleasantly. "Besides which, the other girl was a party-crasher and she started it."

Willie shrugged, brushing Emma off like a flea.

"She's right," Carrie added. "Let her back in."

"Yeah, let her in," everyone around Willie started saying.

"Let Sam in! Let Sam in!" Emma began to chant.

Carrie took one look at Emma's determined face, and joined in. "Let Sam in! Let Sam in!"

Now all around them, kids were taking up the chant. "Let Sam in! Let Sam in!"

Suddenly there was a huge commotion at the front door. Carrie was sure it was Sam, saved from purgatory.

But she was wrong. Sure, Sam slipped in the door, but it was only because Willie and everyone else's attention was riveted to the disheveled figure who had just run in ahead of her.

It was Graham.

Immediately he was surrounded by avid fans, crowding in next to him.

"Graham came?" Emma asked Carrie. "Alone?"

Carrie stared at the mob scene in confusion. Graham hardly ever went out on the island, and he absolutely never went out alone for fear of a scene just like this. "I don't get it—" Carrie began.

"Carrie!" Graham was screaming over the incredible noise of the crowd, craning his neck to find her. "Carrie!"

"What's wrong?" Carrie yelled, fighting her way to him. "Are the kids okay?"

"Of course the kids are okay!" Graham yelled back at her, catching her up in a bear hug. "It's you!"

"Me?" Carrie asked, completely confused.

"You!" Graham yelled triumphantly, picking her up and twirling her around in a circle. "You don't have to get married!"

THIRTEEN

"What?" Carrie asked when Graham finally put her down. "Of course I do!"

A crowd of people gathered around them. Just about everyone at the party knew that Carrie worked for Graham Perry. Someone turned off the music, and a hush fell over the crowd as they waited to see what Graham would say.

"It's over!" Graham yelled, taking Carrie by the shoulders.

"What's over?" Carrie asked. "What are you talking about?"

"The coup, Carrie, the coup!" Graham grinned broadly.

A tiny fissure of hope worked it's way into

Carrie's heart. "Wh . . . what?" she asked shakily.

"There's been an invasion of Matalan, from Colombia," Graham explained. "The U.S. is involved, too. I just heard it on the news!"

Carrie just stood there, too shocked to speak.

"Hey, somebody turn on CNN!" a voice in the crowd screamed.

Carrie simply could not move. Somebody was fumbling with the remote control for the large TV that hung over the room. *Oh my God,* she thought, *her eyes closed tightly. If he's got it right, then I don't have to marry Ray. Oh please, oh please, oh please* . . .

When Carrie opened her eyes and looked up at the TV screen, she saw a huge map of South America with Matalan marked, then enlarged, behind the newscaster.

"To repeat our top story," the anchorwoman said, "the nations of Colombia and Venezuela have announced that democracy has been restored to the tiny island nation of Matalan, following a coordinated military strike by their armed forces, which was supported by air cover from the American aircraft carrier *Independence*. For more on this story, we go to—"

The rest of the story was drowned out by a huge cheer in the Play Café, followed by pandemonium.

"Oh Carrie! I'm so happy for you!" Emma cried, giving Carrie a huge hug.

"Girlfriend! You're a free woman!" Sam whooped, throwing herself at Carrie.

"It's true, isn't it?" Carrie whispered. "It's really true?"

Someone cranked the music back up even louder than before. Everyone was screaming, cheering, laughing, and running up to Carrie to kiss her or shake her hand.

Carrie still couldn't move. She was too afraid to believe in her last-minute reprieve. *This can't actually be happening,* Carrie thought. *I must be dreaming. Yes, this is a dream.*

Then she thought of one way to see whether she was dreaming or not. Oblivious to the people trying to get her attention, and to Graham, who was still talking to her, Carrie pushed her way through the crowd and jumped on a chair, scanning the Play Café for Ray.

She saw him. He was leaning against a pillar, his face turned up to the TV screen. Tears covered his face, but his eyes were shining like the morning sun.

It's true, Carrie thought. *Oh my God. It's really true.* She jumped off the chair and ran for her friend.

"Ray?"

He turned to her, the most beautiful smile on his lips. "Carrie," he said joyfully. "I can go home."

She hugged him tightly and they cried together, until Carrie felt a tap on her shoulder. It was Sam.

"Uh, enough with the water works," Sam barked. "You two are getting soooo boring with all this crying stuff."

"God, I need a tissue," Carrie sniffed, laughing and crying at the same time.

"Well, go find one," Sam said. "And unhand that fine ex-fiancé of yours. It's party time!" Sam dragged Ray on to the dance floor before he could protest.

Carrie made her way to the ladies' room—which took forever because people kept stopping her to congratulate her. Finally she got across the room and practically ran into a empty stall, locking the door behind her. She just had to have a moment alone.

She stood there, her head pressed against the cool door, her eyes closed. The pulsing bass line of the loud music made the door vibrate, and outside the stall girls were chattering and fixing their makeup in front of the mirror. She threw her head back and stared at the ceiling, where someone had scrawled RK IS GONNA GRADOOWATE THIS YEAR FOR SURE, I HOPE.

Carrie laughed out loud. "Good for you, RK!" she cried. "Anything is possible!"

"Hey, Carrie!" someone called, knocking on the stall. "You in there? It's me, Darcy."

"I'll be right out," Carrie called, blowing her nose loudly.

"I'm just delivering a message from Billy,"

Darcy said. "He's waiting for you behind the café."

"Thanks," Carrie said.

"Sure," Darcy replied easily. "Hey, I am so happy for you!" she added. Then Carrie heard the door to the ladies' room open as Darcy left.

Carrie came out of the stall and quickly washed her face and brushed her hair. Then she plowed through the crowd toward the back door of the café. She scanned the deck where people were dancing, eating, drinking and carrying on. No Billy.

She walked down the steps that led to the beach. A warm hand reached for her and pulled her under the porch. Without a word she was in Billy's arms.

"Oh, Billy . . ."

"Shhhh," Billy whispered. "Everything is perfect."

She felt his heart beating against hers, and she didn't need to say a word.

"Please Willie," Sam wheedled, "let the three of us hang here for a while. We'll leave when the cleanup crew is done."

It was almost four o'clock in the morning, and Carrie, Emma, and Sam were still at the Play Café. The party had lasted until three-thirty—way after the usual closing time—when the owner of the café had finally kicked everybody out. Even Ray had left—after passionately being kissed by just about every girl in the place at least once.

"I don't know," Willie said. "The boss won't like it. . . ."

"Hey, you owe me one," Sam pointed out. "You threw me out of my own party."

"Okay," Willie relented with a laugh. "Between you and me, that De Witt broad had it coming to her, anyway." He winked at Sam and lumbered out of the café.

"Tell me that wasn't the party of a lifetime," Sam said, lying across the seat of their usual booth.

"What a night!" Emma said, smiling happily.

"It was unbelievable," Carrie agree, sprawling in a chair.

"Really, it was the single most satisfying

moment of my young life," Sam said with relish.

"When the news report came on?" Emma asked.

"What news report?" Sam joked. "I'm talking about when I launched my drink at Diana De Witt's smug mug!"

"It was great!" Carrie shrieked with laughter.

"Truly satisfying," Emma agreed.

"You're still going to have to sing next to her in the band, though," Carrie reminded her friend.

"It'll be a pleasure," Sam replied. "Every time I look at her I'll think of her with green goop sliding into her bra." The girls cracked up.

"I'm exhausted," Carrie said, laying her head down on the table. She picked up a strand of hair. "Even my hair is exhausted."

"But you feel great too, don't you?" Emma asked.

"Oh yeah," Carrie sighed happily. "You know what was the weirdest part of the whole thing?"

Both Emma and Sam looked at her and shook their heads.

"It was all those people coming up to me tonight—'Oh Carrie, you are so courageous.' 'Oh Carrie, I could never do what you're doing.' 'Oh Carrie, you are such a good person.'" Carrie shook her head. "I felt like a total fraud!"

"How come?" Sam asked.

"Well, it's not like I knew for sure whether I was doing the right thing or not!" Carrie exclaimed, lifting her head from the table. "And it's not like I totally *wanted* to do it."

"Mmmm, I see your point," Sam said.

"I guess there are some things that you just don't know until you do them," Emma said.

"But here's what really gets me," Carrie said emphatically. "I agonized about marrying Ray, I mean, really agonized. I put my friends and my family through all this agony with me—"

"We know, we know," Sam teased.

"And then I finally make up my mind, which is even more agony, and then the whole thing gets turned upside down while I watch TV!"

"Sort of surreal, huh?" Emma commented.

"Totally," Carrie agreed. "I feel like . . ." she searched for the right image, "like a little leaf in a big wind."

"Well," Sam mused, watching the clean-up crew mop the Play Café's floor, "there's just some stuff out there that's bigger than you. Bigger than me even, hard as that might be to believe!"

"But it isn't fair!" Carrie protested. "Ray and I went through such hell—"

"—Sort of for nothing?" Sam finished for her.

"Right," Carrie said. "If we could have known the future, we'd have skipped all that pain!"

"Well, no one ever knows the future," Sam said philosophically. "Oh, except maybe Darcy."

"It's funny," Emma mused, slipping her feet out of her shoes and curling them up underneath her. "I thought a lot about what you decided to do. And I learned that where you draw the line and where I draw the line aren't exactly the same, and that maybe I ought to think again about where I draw the line."

Carrie was puzzled. "What do you mean?"

"I mean," Emma said, "that while I hate to admit it, I don't think if I were you I would have agreed to marry Ray. But I think now, in retrospect, you may have been right."

"Meanwhile," Sam said, "I'm starting to think that you were probably wrong."

Carrie rolled her eyes. "Oh great!" she said with a laugh. "That's *so* helpful!"

"Anyway, you are free, smart, young, and you've got a set of hooters I'd kill for—" Sam began.

"God, you're terrible!" Carrie screeched.

"What say we sneak some Cokes and drink to your freedom?" Sam suggested, crawling out of the booth.

"Can I join the toast?" asked a familiar male voice.

It was Billy Sampson.

"Well, hi!" Sam greeted him, kissing his cheek. "I thought the front door was locked."

"Nope," Billy said. He stared lovingly at Carrie. "How about if I steal you away?"

"What a great idea," Carrie said, going to him.

"Unbelievably mushy," Sam said to Emma, as Carrie and Billy headed for the door.

"Oh Sam, shut up," Emma said good-naturedly.

Billy and Carrie walked hand-in-hand along the water's edge, listening to the low-tide waves slapping gently at the shore. The near dawn was beginning to show on the horizon. Birds squawked to each other and made lazy circles in the still darkened sky.

"You know, Carrie, I don't think I realized how much I loved you until all this happened," Billy said to Carrie softly, as they walked along slowly.

"But you do understand why I was going to do it?" Carrie asked him.

"Why what? Why you were willing to marry him?"

Carrie nodded. "Mmm-hmmm."

Billy bent down and picked up a shell, and

threw it out into the water. "Yeah," he finally said. "I told you that before."

"Well, tell me again," Carrie said. "Please."

Billy sighed. "You were going to marry him because you thought you had to," he said finally, "because otherwise you couldn't live with yourself."

"That was part of it," Carrie said.

"What's the other part?" Billy asked.

"I thought," Carrie said, "when I was trying to decide, what *you* would have done—if it were me, I mean."

"You mean you thought that—"

"I thought that you would have stood by me," Carrie said, "so I thought I should stand by Ray."

Billy stopped walking and turned Carrie toward him. There was a half-smile on his face.

"What if you were wrong?" Billy asked.

"Then I would have made the same decision anyway," Carrie answered matter-of-factly.

"Carrie," Billy said, taking her in his arms. "The last week has been one of the hardest weeks of my life."

"Mine too," Carrie said.

"I know that," Billy responded. "Harder for you than for me. But hard for me too."

Carrie nodded.

"It was like there was no right answer," Billy said.

"I know," Carrie agreed. "No matter what I did, something felt awful."

"I think Pres calls that being caught between a rock and a hard place," Billy said, a smile on his lips.

"Such a colorful guy," Carrie said with a laugh.

"I used to think that there was always a right and wrong in life, you know?" Billy asked, holding her tight.

"Me too," Carrie said. "It would be so much easier . . ."

"I will always admire you for the decision you made," Billy said slowly. "But I hope you won't hate me if I tell you that I wouldn't have done what you did."

She searched his eyes in the half-light. "Meaning if it was me you wouldn't have married me?"

"I am *so* not ready for marriage," Billy said.

"Even if it would save my life?" Carrie pressed.

"If I really believed it was the only way to save your life, I hope I would," Billy said hesitantly. "I'd like to think that I'd do the right thing. . . . God, you must hate me now."

"I don't," Carrie said firmly. "I couldn't. And believe me, I'm no more ready for marriage than you are."

"Carrie Alden, you are the greatest," Billy said, holding her tightly. "I want things to go back to being just how they were before."

Carrie looked up into Billy's blue eyes. "That's not possible, Billy."

A look of alarm flitted across his face. "Why not?"

"Because it did happen, and we're changed by everything that happens to us," Carrie said simply.

"Changed how?" Billy asked.

"Hell if I know," Carrie said with a laugh. "Older and wiser, maybe." She looked up at his beautiful face. "And very much in love, right?"

His only answer was to press his warm lips against hers, and to hold her tight, until the last of the night became a new day.

It was everything.

SUNSET ISLAND MAILBOX

Dear Cherie,

Hello! I absolutely love the Sunset books. I've read them all. I feel like I know everyone from Katie Hewitt to Pres. I know you base Jeff Hewitt on your husband, but are any of the characters based on you? I can't wait to read Sunset After Dark!

> *Your #1 Fan,*
> *Jennifer L. Early*
> *Westfield, New Jersey*

Dear Jennifer,

I asked my friends which Sunset character is most like me, and they told me it's definitely Sam. Personally, I think I'm more a combination of Carrie and Sam. I'm definitely not Emma—I could never be that perfect!

> Best,
> Cherie

Dear Cherie,

You're a terrific writer and I have read all your Sunset books and am planning to read your Sunset After Dark. *One thing bothers me, though. How come Diana and Lorell get away with their horrible comments thrown at Sam, Emma and Carrie? I hate when the enemy gets away with what they want!*

> *Yours truly,*
> *Shayndi Weinraub*
> *Far Rockaway, New York*

Dear Shayndi,

I hate it when the enemy gets away with what they want, too! So . . . what do the rest of you think? Send me ideas for really great ways that Sam, Emma and Carrie can finally put Lorell and Diana in their place! I'll try to use the best idea in a future book!

Best,
Cherie

Dear Cherie,

Sunset Island is the very best book I ever read! Could you make Sunset Island into a movie? I know that zillions of teens would go see Sunset Island in the movies because they hate to read books!

Thanks,
Christy Nicole Kromer
Joshua, Texas

Dear Christy,

Yeah, you're right, a lot of teens don't read much. I think this is really a shame, because a great book allows you to use your imagination in ways that TV and movies don't. However . . . I think your idea of having Sunset Island become a movie is a terrific one! What do the rest of you think?

Best,
Cherie

Dear All,

Hi! Great to see you all again! This is a really busy and exciting time for me. A play I wrote and directed, <u>Candy Store Window</u>, just opened here in Nashville to really fantastic reviews! It's a play about teens, and I wish you all could see it. Many teens show up at the theater with Sunset Island books for me to autograph—which is so cool!

A lot of you write asking me to send you my picture. You can find one in the back of the book. And listen, I absolutely <u>love</u> getting photos of you! In fact, in my office I have a huge map of the U.S.A. covered with photos you've sent me. So <u>pleeeaaasse</u> keep them coming.

As always, I think you are absolutely the greatest and most terrific people in the world. Your letters are wonderful and I will continue to answer each and every letter that you send me. Just be patient—you'll hear from me!

See you on the island!

Best—

Cherie Bennett

Cherie Bennett
c/o General Licensing Company
24 West 25th Street
New York, New York 10010

GOT A TERRIFIC IDEA FOR A SUNSET ISLAND STORY? MAIL IT IN! IF YOUR STORY IDEA IS THE WINNER, CHERIE BENNETT WILL TURN IT INTO AN ACTUAL BOOK--AND YOU WILL WIN A FREE TRIP TO MEET HER IN NASHVILLE, TENNESSEE! 100 RUNNERS-UP WILL RECEIVE A SUNSET ISLAND T-SHIRT!

No purchase necessary. See below for complete details.

SUNSET ISLAND™ SUMMER '93 CONTEST RULES

GRAND PRIZE: Grand Prize winner's story idea will be the basis of a future Sunset Island novel. Round-trip transportation for Grand Prize winner and one legal guardian to Nashville, Tennessee; a two-night stay at a hotel, including all meals (but not including personal expenses, i.e. laundry, telephone calls); dinner with Cherie Bennett, author of the SUNSET ISLAND novels published by The Berkley Publishing Group.

100 RUNNERS-UP: A Sunset Island T-shirt

NO PURCHASE NECESSARY.

1. All entries must be clearly printed or typewritten. On the upper left-hand corner of an 8½" x 11" sheet of paper, put your name, address, telephone number, and date of birth. On the same piece of paper, in your own words, typewritten, or clearly printed, in one hundred words or less, write your own original plot idea, centering around any one or all three of these Sunset Island characters: Emma, Sam, and/or Carrie.

2. Entry must be postmarked no later than September 30, 1993. Not responsible for lost or misdirected mail. The winner and runners-up will be announced and notified by mail by January 15, 1994.

3. Entrant must be 17 years of age or younger. One entry per person. Entry is property of General Licensing Company, Inc. and will not be returned. The grand prize is the sole compensation for the winning entry. No substitution of prizes is permitted. Travel must be completed by August 31, 1994. Travel and accommodation dates subject to availability.

4. This contest is open to all residents of the continental U.S. seventeen years of age and younger. Void where prohibited by law. Employees and their families of The Putnam Berkley Group, MCA, Matsushita Electrical & Industrial Corporation, General Licensing Company, Inc., their respective affiliates, retailers, distributors, advertising, promotion, and production agencies are not eligible.

5. Taxes on all prizes are the sole responsibility of the prize-winner whose legal guardian may be required to sign and return a statement of eligibility within fourteen days of notification. Winner must assign all rights in the plot to General Licensing Company, Inc. The names and likenesses of the winner and the guardian may be used for promotional purposes.

6. In the event there are an insufficient number of entries that meet the minimum requirements of the judge, the sponsor reserves the right not to award all prizes.

7. Mail entries to: SUNSET ISLAND CONTEST
c/o General Licensing Company, Inc.
24 West 25th Street
New York, NY 10010

8. For the name of the grand prize winner, send a stamped, self-addressed envelope to SUNSET ISLAND CONTEST WINNER, c/o General Licensing Company, Inc., 24 West 25th Street, New York, NY 10010

Sunset Island is a trademark of General Licensing Company, Inc.